BLUE HEARTS

Also by Jim Lehrer

Books

A Bus of My Own
Short List
Lost and Found
The Sooner Spy
Crown Oklahoma
Kick the Can
We Were Dreamers
Viva Max!

Plays

The Will and Bart Show
Church Key Charlie Blue
Chili Queen

A Novel

BLUE HEARTS

Jim Lehrer

RANDOM HOUSE
New York

Copyright © 1993 by Jim Lehrer

All rights reserved under International and Pan-American Copyright Conventions.
Published in the United States by Random House, Inc., New York, and simultaneously
in Canada by Random House of Canada Limited, Toronto.

Library of Congress Cataloging-in-Publication Data

Lehrer, James.
      Blue hearts: a novel / Jim Lehrer.
          p.   cm.
      ISBN 0-679-42216-1
      I. Title.
    PS3562.E4419B58   1993
    813'.54—dc20   92-37167

Book design by Tanya M. Pérez

Manufactured in the United States of America
98765432
First Edition

To Robin

PART ONE

Charlie

October 7–14, 1990

C harlie's train was at 9:35. He awoke on his own just before 8:00 and ordered a continental breakfast from room service. A danish, a hard roll, orange juice and coffee. He also asked them to bring along a *Washington Post*. A morning that did not start with the *Post* was a rare and deprived morning for Charlie. He read everything in the paper except the Style section, which, except for the art and book criticism, he considered to be mostly overwritten, overblown gossip and drivel. Mary Jane strongly disagreed and always read Style first and thoroughly.

Increasingly, it was the obituaries in the back of the Metro section that interested Charlie the most. Seldom a day went by that he did not read about the demise of someone he knew or worked with at the Agency, usually from emphysema or throat or lung cancer. In the early days, all spies of all ranks and talents from all countries and interests were chain smokers. Charlie was always amused about the fact that he and most American agents smoked Gauloises, Gitanes and other French brands, while he seldom met a European operator, East or West, who smoked anything other than American-made Marlboros.

The obits sometimes made him sad but they always made him angry. None of them ever had the real story about what the guy had done for the government and people of the United States. In fact, he was still annoyed about the case of Jack Douglas.

Jack was the CIA officer who thought of the idea of smuggling the manuscripts of Pasternak, Solzhenitsyn and other great Russian novelists out of the Soviet Union for publication in the West. It was a great psychological warfare victory that drove the KGB up the wall. But when Jack Douglas had died twelve days ago, his modest obituary said only that he had been a career intelligence officer with the Central Intelligence Agency. There was not a word about the book triumph. Charlie had gone to Jack's funeral and it wasn't talked of publicly there either.

Charlie had even mentioned it to Bruce Conn Clark. They had run into each other on the night of Jack's funeral at DeCarlo's, a restaurant in the Spring Valley section of Northwest Washington. Clark was the former secretary of state who had also been a young warrior intelligence officer in the 1960s. Charlie had worked with him briefly on a special assignment after the assassination of President John F. Kennedy.

Charlie thought again of Jack Douglas and of who might have died today in the *Post* before stepping into the shower. He had brought only a clean sports shirt and a change of socks and underwear for the brief overnight trip into Washington for the Brookings Institution dinner symposium on economic intelligence gathering in the post–Cold War world.

He was dressed and waiting when the room-service waiter knocked on the door, a pleasant young black man in a white coat who spoke in broken but precise English. Ethiopia, thought Charlie. Maybe the Sudan. Charlie was good at that kind of ID. It was another of those things he did almost automatically out of habit.

The waiter placed the tray on a small conversation table in one corner of the room. Charlie only glanced at it and signed the check. And the waiter left. Charlie sat down, poured himself a cup of coffee from the silver coffeepot and then noticed something was missing. The newspaper. Where was the *Post?* Damn!

He went to the door, hoping to catch the waiter. He was gone. Charlie thought about calling back to room service. No, to hell with it. He felt in his pocket to make sure the room key was there and closed the door. I'll go get a paper downstairs myself.

The elevator was ten or so room doors down the hall. He arrived, pushed the down button.

A tremendous explosion rocked him backward and almost knocked him down. He looked back. Smoke was pouring out of a room some ten or so doors up the hall.

———————————

So Charlie went home to West Virginia on the 2:35 train. He went without his dirty clothes and his small overnight bag and shaving kit. They were all destroyed in the explosion and fire. When he called Mary Jane to tell her of the change in travel plans he told her somebody had stolen his bag. She had spent all of her married life with worries about awful possibilities that went with her husband's work and there was no need to bring them out of retirement. Not yet, at least.

And, most important, he had never before told her when he was really scared. He was certainly not going to start now.

The train was less than half full, so he had no one next to him, no one to distract him from the scenery or his thoughts. Charlie loved the train ride to and from Washington. The states of Maryland and West Virginia ran it as a subsidized commuter train seventy-five miles up the Potomac River to Martinsburg. It was early October, his favorite time of the year everywhere, but particularly on the train. The trees were red and yellow and purple, the sky was a soft, clean blue and the combination always reminded

Charlie of a quilt his grandmother had on her bed in Joplin. Joplin, Missouri, was where Charlie was born, grew up and got much of what was in him that was important.

His thoughts. Detective Sergeant Linwood Bock of the Metropolitan D.C. Police was in them for a while. Charlie had always been partial to cops because he felt they and schoolteachers were the only real daily heroes in America. But on a one-to-one basis cops could be difficult to handle; the better they were, the harder. Bock, a Vietnam vet in his forties with a west North Carolina accent, was one of those. He would not accept Charlie's line that he had no idea why somebody would bomb his hotel room. In the old days Charlie would simply have given him a name and number to call. That name and number would have supplied whatever information Bock needed to quit asking questions. That option was not available anymore. Charlie deflected Bock for the time being, but he knew he would be back after laboratory test results were available and some more interviewing of the room-service waiter and other hotel employees was completed.

Charlie went through the possibilities, beginning with the one he tried to peddle to Bock. Mistaken identity. The bomb was meant for somebody other than me, a retired government bureaucrat about to catch a train back to his peaceful life as an innkeeper in the panhandle of West Virginia. Bock clearly did not buy it.

What Bock did or did not buy was the least of it. What did he, Charlie himself, buy? Could it have been a mistake? Could he dare believe it was a mistake? The intended victim was not Charlie Henderson, oh, no, not Charlie Henderson.

But on the other hand, what if it was no mistake? That blown-up breakfast tray was meant to be mine. So who would want me dead?

He ran through the current "consultancies" he was doing for the Agency. One had to do with helping the new Hungarian government determine which of their old Communist government's intelligence officers should be fired, retired or indicted. Another was nothing more than looking at a few organizational charts for Philippine intelligence to see if a planned reorganization made sense.

Neither had any protruding sticklers that he could think of. They were mostly boring, in fact. But everything in this new post–Cold War world of the Agency seemed boring to him. All of it made him so grateful he had come into the spy business when he did, when there were real enemies, real things to be done, real adventures to be had. Protecting Microsoft's software secrets from the Koreans and Taiwanese, as they were talking about at the Brookings thing, was not Charlie's idea of a good time, or of a life, for that matter.

He Rolodexed backward casually and lightly with hops and skips through his thirty-five years as an intelligence officer for the United States of America. He had been both covert and overt, both operational and administrative. He had served overseas in Europe, Southeast Asia and Latin America and had held many jobs that were headquartered in or run right out of Langley. Nothing came to mind. Sure, there were some tricky times and there were some enemies made. But nothing that he could think of that would cause somebody to bomb his breakfast at the Hyatt Regency on Capitol Hill now.

The train sounded its whistle. Duffields, his stop, was next. Duffields was only a small country store, a few houses, a gravel parking lot for commuters' cars and two churches—a trim historic Episcopalian one for whites, a run-down white frame AME for blacks. There was no train station and the train stopped in the middle of the blacktop road for passengers to get on or off. Tickets had to be bought from the conductor.

He saw Mary Jane waiting for him alongside their Jeep Wagoneer.

———

"Let's walk the track," Charlie said within minutes after they pulled away from Duffields. Mary Jane smiled. That was her way of saying, Sure, Charlie. There was a Chessie Railroad branch track that ran through the front of their property. Every morning around eleven o'clock a train of ten to twelve freight cars went slowly by west, and then in the afternoon around four o'clock another one about the same size came back east. Walking up and down the track through some nearby wetlands was Charlie's favorite form of exercise and relaxation. Mary Jane preferred tennis, but she didn't mind walking with Charlie and he didn't mind playing tennis with her. It was their life together.

"We now have two bookings for Friday night," she said as she drove the Wagoneer down Highway 231, the windy two-lane blacktop, toward Charles Town. "A third called for Saturday. A couple from Harrisburg, Pennsylvania. So we'll have six for dinner," Mary Jane said. "Maybe you could shoot up to Martinsburg for some more brandy snifters?"

"Tomorrow, you bet," said Charlie. "I'll put them on the list."

Theoretically, their bed-and-breakfast was open seven days a week, but as a practical matter it was mostly a weekend place. That was when people from Washington and Baltimore could come to spend some quiet time in the country of West Virginia. Their operation was also not technically just a bed-and-breakfast. On Saturday nights there was always a black-tie dinner for the guests, fully catered and served by Wes and Paul, two young men from Shepherdstown, one of them a former chef at the Greenbriar resort hotel in White Sulphur Springs, West Virginia. They brought with them fine wine, exotic desserts and three young women in white dresses from the music faculty at Shepherd College to play string music during dinner. It was part of a high-class weekend designed by Mary Jane to make staying at their place more than simply special.

Mary Jane Lawrence Henderson was the same age as Charlie and in every other way his equal. Her hair was gray but her body was thin, tight, brown like Charlie's. Her mind was active and quick and she was of a Nantucket and Needham, Massachusetts, breed that was at home and at peace with themselves and in almost any situation.

Charlie and Mary Jane Henderson's eighteenth-century house

was called Hillmont. It was a Georgian manor house of red Dutch brick that had eight huge rooms with a fireplace in each, huge hallways, three smaller stone outbuildings and a history that included at least one meal of George Washington's. George's brother Samuel lived two miles down the road from Hillmont, and on a trip to see him George stopped for dinner at Hillmont, then owned by an old friend of his. That was on March 10, 1771, and George wrote it up in his diary. Charlie went to the Library of Congress, found the exact notation in George's own hand, had a copy made, blew it up a little bit and put it in a frame which he then hung on a wall inside the house. Said George: "Dined at Mr. Nurses & returned to my Brother's in the Evening." Hardly Declaration of Independence material and short on detail, but Charlie and Mary Jane's paying guests loved it.

Charlie had found the house through a former Agency clandestine type who sold real estate in Shepherdstown, which was fifteen miles north of Hillmont and, along with Charles Town, Martinsburg and Harpers Ferry, formed a thirty-square-mile cluster of towns, roads, fields and streams full of Civil War as well as colonial history. The real estate guy was Jay Buckner, whom Charlie had known mostly around the edges in the Congo, Laos and other places as someone with special skills in the so-called technical services—electronics, armaments, communications. He got the boot in the so-called Schlesinger purge following the Church Committee investigations of the Agency in 1974. Buckner had almost single-handedly turned the panhandle of West Virginia into a little haven for ex-Agency types with a desire for the good country life near Washington at a price and pace second to the toney hunt country around Middleburg, fifty miles south in Virginia. The word was out that Buckner was also working "secretly" with one of the United States senators from West Virginia to bring part of CIA headquarters out to a five-hundred-acre spot only ten miles from Hillmont. Charlie and Mary Jane had joined the effort to keep it out of the area.

Hey, what about that? Maybe Buckner was trying to kill him for standing in the way of his big real estate deal? Oh, come on, Charlie.

Mary Jane showed him the menu that was being planned for the weekend. For Saturday night dinner, some chicken patties alleged to have been a favorite of Martha Washington, French oxtail broth, veal with mushrooms, salad, white peach ice cream and two good wines, a white and a red. For breakfast the next morning, shad roe sautéed in brown butter and lemon, quail braised with lardons and port wine sauce, eggs scrambled with truffles, apple fritters, a cured ham, grits with Asiago cheese and all kinds of fruits and tarts. The boys from Shepherdstown had come up with another winner. Those two meals, plus three lighter ones and two nights' lodging, came to $450 a person. Expensive but worth every penny.

"I can hardly wait to eat this stuff," Charlie said.

"It's not stuff, Charlie," Mary Jane said. "It's elegance."

Charlie had continued his burglar lie about how he lost his shaving kit and other clothes. After about fifteen or so minutes on the railroad track Mary Jane suddenly but quietly said, "When will you tell me what really happened?"

Mary Jane's unerring skill at seeing through him continued to startle her husband. He was sure she was the only one who could. "Soon," he said. "Soon."

"Is it something serious?"

"No, no."

"Official?"

"I don't think so."

Charlie had changed to his favorite walking outfit that included a pair of faded dark green corduroy pants, scuffed cordovan boots and a red, green and dark blue striped cotton sweater. He had a collection of more than twenty walking sticks. He had chosen one they had picked up at the Portobello antique market in London shortly after they bought Hillmont. The handle was a hard ivory head of a cocker spaniel. Mary Jane was already dressed for walking.

The cattails in the wetlands were still out. So were some of the late wildflowers, small pink and purple and yellow things that were difficult to cut because of their prickly stems. Walking the track meant awkwardly stretched strides from one wooden tie to the next. Charlie, who was just over six feet tall and had long legs, loved the rhythm of left-right, left-right. Mary Jane was five inches shorter than Charlie, which meant shorter legs and the constant possibility that she would miss the next tie and fall flat on her face.

"Don't do anything crazy, Charlie," she said, her eyes downward, intent on the business of walking without tripping. "Remember your age, please."

"Remember what Po Chü-i said, please," he said, his eyes looking off to the right at the back of the marvelous white main house and outbuildings of Altona Farm, another eighteenth-century masterpiece still standing and alive in the twentieth century.

Po Chü-i was a Chinese poet who lived from the year 772 until 846. When he turned sixty in 832 he wrote a poem about it. An old friend had sent it to Charlie on his sixtieth birthday and Charlie had taken it as his life's creed.

Saith Po Chü-i, in part:

> Between thirty and forty, one is distracted by the Five Lusts; between seventy and eighty one is prey to a hundred diseases. But from sixty to seventy one is free from all ills. Calm and still—the heart enjoys rest. I have put behind me Love and Greed. I have done with Profit and Fame. I am still short of illness and decay and far from decrepit age. Strength of limb I still possess to see the rivers and hills. Still my heart has spirit enough to listen to flutes and strings. At leisure I open new wine and taste several cups; drunken I recall old poems and sing a whole volume.

———

Martinsburg, twenty minutes north of Charles Town on State Highway 9, was where Charlie and Mary Jane did most of their heavy shopping. That was because of something called the Blue Ridge Outlet Center, a collection of some fifty stores with well-known names in three old buildings that had been woolen factories in their first lives. Ralph Lauren, J. Crew, Country Road, Benetton, London Fog, Levi's, Corning and Adidas were among the companies who now used them to sell irregular and overstocked merchandise at deeply discounted prices.

Charlie's list was a short one and he planned to be back at Hillmont by noon. It was just after ten-thirty when he parked the Wagoneer in the small lot west of the main building. He almost always did that so he could walk by the tables of irregular knit shirts in the Ralph Lauren store to see what they had in extra-large. Most of them were under twenty dollars and, even though some had tiny holes and rips, they were great for rough wear or playing tennis. The only problem was the guy on the polo pony, the symbol of Ralph Lauren that was on most of the shirts. Charlie thought it was ridiculous to be a walking human billboard for Ralph Lauren or anyone else, so he had a policy against buying or wearing anything with a symbol on it. The trick was to find those few shirts that didn't have it.

He found one almost immediately for nineteen dollars. It was bright orange with a blue collar. The irregular problem was a black smudge on the left breast pocket. He folded it up to take to the cash register when he realized what he had left in the Wagoneer. The list. He had left the list of what he was supposed to buy there on the dashboard.

He put the shirt back on the table and headed for the door. His eyes went to the Wagoneer. A man in a dark green sweater and a white baseball cap was walking away from it. He was carrying a dark brown leather attaché case, not a shopping bag. Charlie watched the man disappear at the far end of the lot and turn left onto the street. There were other cars in the lot; he had probably come from one of those cars. But there was something about the way he walked that was familiar. It could be anybody from around here, thought Charlie. He and Mary Jane had gotten to know a lot of people. And yet there was something about him that made that seem unlikely, something that sounded an alarm in Charlie. A chilling alarm.

Operating on reflex, he moved back away from the door, stayed inside and watched his Wagoneer and the parking lot. He watched for two or three minutes, feinting an anxiety over a late appointment for the clerks at the nearby cash register. Somebody, probably his wife, was supposed to have met him at the west entrance into Ralph Lauren's and was running late. Isn't that the way it always was?

The man did not return. Nothing happened. Charlie went out to the Wagoneer. Okay, now what? Is there a bomb hooked up to the ignition or to a door? Has a brake line been cut? Will the steering explode the first time I turn a corner? Has a front tire been programmed to blow going around a curve?

Charlie decided he was crazy even to think like this. My God almighty, he lectured himself. Yes, Charlie, but that bomb at the Hyatt was God almighty real. Be careful, be smart, be alive.

He unlocked the front driver's side door and opened it. Nothing happened. He leaned in, reached over and grabbed Mary Jane's list. Nothing happened. He closed the door and relocked it. Nothing happened.

But as he turned to walk away he smelled something. It was the smell of freshly cut rubber. He checked all four tires for cuts or indentations. There was a technique Charlie knew about that involved sticking into a tire small sharp pieces of metal that could be geared to the tire's revolutions to cause a blowout when the car hit fifty miles per hour or more. It was also possible to put little detonator caps on those pieces of metal to speed the process along.

He found nothing on the four tires. Rubber? How about a hose? He went around to the front and opened the hood. All the hoses seemed in place, firm and normal. But then, as he was about to close the hood, he noticed that one of the four was a slightly darker shade of black. Meaning it was newer. The Wagoneer was less than a year old. He knew he had not had any hoses replaced and he doubted Mary Jane would have without telling him.

It took him only a minute or two to discover that the new hose ran from the carburetor up to and into the heating and air-conditioning vents. So, after a few minutes of driving with the windows up, he, the driver, would be overcome with carbon monoxide fumes, pass out and cause the Wagoneer to crash.

He ripped out the hose and then looked around. Somebody was certain to be sitting off in a car somewhere watching him. But he could not spot anybody. They're probably on binoculars, he thought. All his survival instincts told him to jump into the Wagoneer and drive away. But what would he tell Mary Jane if he came home with nothing? He took out the list. Four brandy snifters, two single white sheets, a commode brush, four ruby-red washcloths, a hanging fern and several packets of plain white paper cocktail napkins, among other things. He needed an idea. And before his eyes came one in the form of two teenage boys walking from their red Toyota pickup toward him.

"How would you guys like to make ten bucks?" he said to the boys.

"We're not into drugs, man," said one of them. Both were black, and both were wearing athletic letter jackets of some kind.

"No drugs," Charlie said. "I just want you to sit in this Wagoneer for fifteen minutes."

"Hey, man, what's the deal?"

"My wife is supposed to meet me here but an emergency has come up and I need to go inside and buy some things. If she comes, you tell her I will be right back."

The two boys exchanged glances.

"We'll do it for five," one of them said to Charlie.

"It's a deal. I'll be right back."

"Payable in advance," the other kid said.

"Three now, two when I get back."

He paid them and went inside, bought everything on the list and was back outside in just over ten minutes. The two kids were still there at the Wagoneer. He gave them two more dollars and drove off feeling slightly smart.

═══════════════

Ten minutes later Charlie gunned the Wagoneer just after going through the traffic light at Kearneysville, the only town on Highway 9 between Martinsburg and Charles Town. He turned the steering wheel to the right to follow a slight curve in the road and nothing happened. The Wagoneer kept going straight ahead. He slammed on the brakes, and the Wagoneer started sliding as it careened off the road into and through a ditch and came to a stop in the front yard of a small white framed house with a Greg Didden Realtors FOR SALE sign in the front yard. He was not hurt. Neither was the Wagoneer.

Oh, Charlie. What a fool you are. The standard procedure was to plant a double hit. The first one is found, the target feels he is safe, lets his guard down, and then comes number-two hit. Rusty, rusty is what I am, thought Charlie, once he said a few words of thanks to Somebody for being alive. And he wondered if this was what Po Chü-i had in mind when he wrote of recalling old poems and singing a whole volume.

It took a mechanic in Kearneysville thirty minutes to repair the power-steering fluid line that he told Charlie looked like it had been sliced in two with a razor blade.

But Charlie did not have to be told that. He was now, finally, on full alert, full smart and full fear.

═══════════════

The call came minutes after Mary Jane left the house. She had gone down to the tennis court for a workout with the electronic ball machine. That machine was her pride and joy. It could be programmed to deliver more than a hundred balls over the net at varying speeds and heights and to different sections of the court.

Bruce Conn Clark's secretary asked if Mr. Henderson was there for Mr. Clark. Yes, ma'am, said Charlie.

"Clark here," Clark said. That was his trademark phone greeting.

There was no small talk.

"It was good seeing you at DeCarlo's the other night, Charlie," said Bruce Conn Clark. "I was thinking about what you said and thought maybe we should talk some more about it."

"About what exactly?" Charlie replied.

"About secrets and the keeping thereof even when they do not seem to matter anymore."

Charlie remembered his saying something like that. "Sure, we can talk about it," he said now. "I think people like Jack Douglas should be honored for what they did, particularly with the coming of *glasnost* and all of that."

"How about tomorrow?"

"Tomorrow?"

"I was supposed to fly to Vienna for a meeting but it was scrubbed."

Bells of unknown origin and sound were clanging in Charlie's head. "I could come in on the late-morning train."

"When does it arrive?"

"Around eleven."

"How about lunch at G Street Club at noon?"

"Deal."

Neither said a real good-bye.

———

Bruce Conn Clark and Charles Avenue Henderson did not live in the same Washington worlds. Bruce had gone on from the

Agency to become one of the world's leading statesmen, and was now an international consultant of great influence and renown. Charlie had gone on to one Agency assignment after another, and was now a retired spook. Lunch at the G Street Club?

What exactly had he said to Clark at DeCarlo's?

Charlie had gone there with Dan Horton, another retired hand from the Soviet Russia Division, who had flown in from Sarasota, Florida, for Jack's funeral. They agreed on DeCarlo's for old time's sake, and Lucy DeCarlo, acting as if she really did remember the two of them, gave them a familiar table in a corner in the back room. Charlie had often gone to DeCarlo's with Mary Jane at night as well as at lunch with other Agency people.

Bruce Conn Clark was already there in an opposite corner at a table with three other men. Charlie's and his eyes met and Charlie went over to the table.

"Secretary Clark, I'm Charlie Henderson," Charlie said, extending his hand. "You may not remember me but we worked together once."

Bruce Conn Clark's famous face was a complete blank. He clearly did not remember Charlie Henderson. Charlie felt like a fool. He quickly said: "November 1963."

Clark's face, known and celebrated for showing nothing, came to life. "Oh, yes. Yes, yes." He stood and really shook Charlie's hand now.

"We were just talking about keeping secrets from the old days," Charlie said, nodding toward Dan Horton, who had already gone on to their table and sat down.

Clark said nothing. Charlie said, "A mutual friend from the Agency died and they had his funeral today. He had done some great things for his country but nobody said a damned thing about them."

"That is too bad," Clark said. "It really is."

That was all that was said, all that happened.

So why did Bruce Conn Clark call him for lunch at the G Street Club? Tomorrow?

Listen to that *Clang! Clang!*, Charlie. What's it mean?

=====

Charlie worked out a plan that he hoped he could maneuver quietly by Mary Jane without alarming her. She bought the first part, which was simply that he had to go back to Washington in the morning to see a guy about a special consultancy project. And she did not seem too concerned when he said he would take their old Ford pickup truck to the station and leave it rather than have her drive him. After all, he told her, he was coming right back that afternoon, so there was no reason for her to bother. Also, it would clear her to worry only about the weekend guests who would be showing up that afternoon.

It was when he said he would pack a bag with some overnight things as a "backup" that she smelled the rat.

"In case the meeting drags on and I miss the train," Charlie said, "I'll be all set to grab a hotel room with no problem."

"What's going on, Charlie?" she asked him directly, the only way she ever asked anybody anything.

"Nothing serious," he lied.

"If it gets serious will you tell me?"

"Sure," he said. "Haven't I always?"

"No."

"Well, this time I will."

Instead of driving the truck to Duffields, where he always caught the train, he drove to Martinsburg, where it originated. He parked the truck in the public lot, locked it and got on the train. Once aboard he took a pair of sunglasses and a red-billed baseball cap that said "Washington Redskins" across the front from his small overnight valise and put them on. It was not a real disguise but it would do what he felt needed to be done.

He found a seat in the last of the four chair cars and opened *The Washington Post* he had picked up at a vending machine at the station. In fourteen minutes exactly the train arrived at Duffields, where he would have been expected to get on.

He looked out the right side of the train. People were getting aboard. He saw the black Methodist Church. Then he looked to the left: Duffields store and the white Episcopal Church. He was not sure what he was looking for, but when he saw it he knew.

Jay Buckner, the former technical-services man who now sold real estate in Shepherdstown, was standing alongside a blue Chevrolet Suburban. He appeared to be watching for someone to arrive.

Jay Buckner was wearing a dark green sweater and a white baseball cap.

Charlie spent some of the next hour and twenty-eight minutes of the train ride wondering what Jay Buckner had had in mind. Was he going to throw me from the train? Derail the train? Blow it up? Hit me with a deadly toxin dart? Slip a letter bomb into the sports section of my *Post?*

Charlie spent only a few minutes focusing on and digesting the fact that Buckner knew ahead of time that Charlie had planned to catch that particular train to Washington.

And the only person who knew that besides Mary Jane was Bruce Conn Clark.

Charlie remained seated when the train pulled into Washington's Union Station. He sat there and worked on the *Post's* crossword puzzle for ten minutes after all the other passengers had disembarked and scattered through the terminal building to taxis, the subway or whatever. He got up and left when a cleaning woman came into the car.

"This really is the end of the line," she said. She was a pleasant overweight black woman of forty or so.

"Sorry," was all Charlie said, folding his paper.

The Maryland/West Virginia commuter trains came in on Track 7, which was in the western half of the station's track slots. The normal way to leave was to walk down the platform and then swing left and follow a walkway into the terminal itself. Charlie, acting like he was fully within his rights, turned right, stepped around a construction barricade and followed another walkway into the terminal, the one used by railroad and construction workers. It brought him into the building next to a restaurant called the American Café and the entrance to the subway, known in Washington as Metro. Only in New York is the subway the subway.

He was reasonably certain no one was on him when he went through the turnstile and jumped aboard the next metro going into downtown. But just in case, he never stopped moving, walking from the first car through the second to the third, where he leaped out as the doors closed. He was at the Farragut Square North Station.

The G Street Club, where he was to meet Bruce Conn Clark, was some ten blocks south and west from where he came out. He took the scenic route down through Lafayette Park to Pennsylvania Avenue, walked by the White House and the Old Executive Office Building to Seventeenth Street, then past G and F to E and then west. He was delighted to see that he had correctly remembered there was a pay phone at E and Twenty-first, two blocks south of the G Street Club at G and Twenty-first.

It was 12:05. He dialed the number of the G Street Club and asked for Mr. Clark. It didn't take long for Bruce Conn Clark to say what he always said: "Clark here."

"Henderson here," Charlie said. "A problem came up, Bruce. I can't make lunch."

"Where are you now?" said Clark. His voice was as strong and straight as usual. But he was clearly annoyed.

"I'm over in Winchester," said Charlie. "I drove the truck over to pick up some roofing stuff for the house. Something sprung a leak up there." Winchester was Winchester, Virginia, a town of ten thousand in the heart of apple country, twenty minutes west of Charles Town and an hour and a half from Washington. "Sorry I didn't have a chance to call earlier."

"No problem. You're missing halibut in a white wine sauce."

"Next time," said Charlie. "Can I have a raincheck until I'm down your way again?"

"Certainly. When will you be coming?"

"Don't know. I'll call first, of course."

"Of course."

Again, there were no formal good-byes.

Charlie walked toward G Street and stopped against a low building. He had a view of the front door of the club, which was a two-story white house frequented mostly by people with money, which in Washington meant mostly lawyers and former cabinet officials who, like Clark, worked for foreign countries and interests. Clark's car and driver were waiting at the curb.

In two or three minutes Bruce Conn Clark walked out and got in. And the car drove off. Charlie almost moved from his spot but something stopped him.

Wait, wait. Be smart.

In two or three more minutes a man came around from the side of the G Street Club and got into a gray Ford sedan that had been parked on the other side of the street. The man was in a dark suit. It was Jay Buckner, a man who clearly knew how to get places fast.

After Buckner drove away Charlie was overcome by a feeling of well-being. He figured it was caused by some of the rust flaking off and falling away. And by a feeling of exhilaration he had not experienced in years. Nine years to be exact.

It was for the game. Could he still play? That was the question. You just watch me, Bruce Conn Clark. Here I come.

━━━━━━━━━

The first call was to Mary Jane. All he said was, "I may be gone for a while, sweetheart."

She said nothing in response and Charlie said, "Did you hear me?"

"Yes," said Mary Jane. "I thought this was over, Charlie. Are you okay?"

"I'm fine."

"Where are you?"

"In Baltimore."

There was silence again. Then Mary Jane said, "Remember the Chinaman poet also saith between sixty and seventy the heart enjoys rest."

"And he also said, 'Still my heart has spirit enough to listen to flutes and strings.' I saith I love you," he said.

"I love you, Charlie," she said. "After all that's happened I'd hate to lose you in retirement."

Charlie was in a room at the Holiday Inn at Tyson's Corner, a huge conglomeration of shopping centers, office buildings and apartments in the Virginia suburb of McLean. He had gone there in a new dark green Plymouth Fury that he had rented from a Budget Rent-A-Car office on K Street in downtown Washington. Tyson's Corner was only twenty minutes from downtown, across Memorial Bridge to the George Washington Parkway and then west on Dolley Madison Boulevard. It was a route that passed right by the Langley headquarters building of the Agency. That proximity was one of several reasons Charlie had chosen that particular Holiday Inn.

His second call was in fact to the CIA. He was put right through to the deputy director, Joshua Eugene Bennett.

"Somebody's trying to kill me, Josh," Charlie said. They had met, as if by accident, in the men's shirt section of Neiman-Marcus at Tyson's Corner II. In loud voices they talked about how long it had been since they had seen each other and they exchanged information about each other's wives and lives. Then, with apparent casualness, they walked together out into the mall and sat down on one of the many wooden benches stationed throughout for shoppers in need of a rest. The bench they chose was next to a fountain that was noisily thrusting water up into the air. Piped-in music was also playing. Charlie was delighted to notice when they sat down that the music was a medley of songs by Ray Conniff and his singers. "How High the Moon," an old Les Paul and Mary Ford song from the forties, was among the first he recognized.

"An angry husband, I assume," Josh said. "Shame on you, you old fart."

Charlie smiled and glanced around at the dress and shoe stores, walk-up orange juice and chocolate chip cookie stands and other enterprises that surrounded them. Nobody seemed to be paying any attention to these two well-dressed men on the bench.

"It's for real and it's serious," Charlie said.

"Who and why?"

"I may know who but I don't know why."

"Who?"

"Maybe Bruce Conn Clark."

Now it was Joshua Eugene Bennett's turn to glance around casually at shoppers and vendors and lights and shop windows.

"You have got to be kidding," he said when he had finished his look around.

"I think it has to do with something we did together years ago."

"With us?"

"Maybe."

"What?"

"I can't say."

"Thanks a lot."

Josh Bennett was ten years younger than Charlie, who was his first friend and mentor in the Agency. He had come with a master's degree in medieval intellectual history directly from Brown University, and became known as a smart, cool comer from the day he arrived. He was a physical opposite of Charlie. He was only five feet nine, always a steady twenty pounds overweight and always losing his hair. He, like Charlie, had held a variety of jobs on the operations side with a specialty in Eastern Europe. At fifty-one and completely bald, he was given the number-two job after the guy who had it fell victim to not asking enough questions about who was running arms and other supplies to the Contras in Nicaragua.

Josh was there when Charlie earned his Blue Heart. That was in West Berlin in 1971. They were involved in a low-level swap of a Czech intelligence officer who had been caught with his fingers in the pants and safe of a male assistant to the military attaché at the Belgian embassy in Bonn. He was being traded for a Chilean businessman who had been caught by the Hungarians with some Warsaw Pact troop-maneuver plans in his briefcase. Neither Charlie nor Josh was running him as an agent, but they were then key players in a small special-operations unit that handled things like swaps and defectors. Charlie was then working undercover as an international banking consultant in London; Josh was in Geneva with real AFL-CIO credentials and duties as a liaison to the world labor movement. The Czech decided at the last minute that he did not want to go back home to the other side. He pulled a thirty-eight and shot Charlie, his sole final escort toward the Glieneker Brucke bridge, in the stomach. He was set to shoot him again but did not count on Josh, who was playing the part of a civilian West German driver. Josh turned around from the front seat and put a thirty-two round right between the eyes of the Czech. It saved Charlie's life but ruined the swap and caused both Josh and Charlie to spend hours being interviewed and reviewed by Agency supervisors and inspectors. Both were finally cleared and praised, and the director at the time gave Charlie the Blue Heart in a ceremony attended only by Charlie and two other Agency officials. Blue Heart was the unofficial in-house name for a citation given in secret to CIA personnel wounded or otherwise injured in the line of duty. Their families got them if they died.

"Now, now, Charlie," Josh said. "It seems hard for me to believe that a man of Bruce Conn Clark's prominence would go around killing people for something that happened years ago. He wasn't even in the Agency that long, was he?"

"Eight or nine years, I think. Why don't you check it out?"

"Charlie, come on now. I look at his 703 File and what do I see?"

"I don't know what you'll see until you see it. That is the point."

"What did the two of you do together?"

Charlie looked away from Josh.

"You might as well tell me, Charlie," Josh said, "because it'll be in that file."

Not necessarily, thought Charlie. He said: "We worked on a Soviet thing."

"The kind of thing that twenty-some years later would turn him into a madog killer of Charlie Henderson?"

"Please look at his file."

"For what?"

"You'll know for what when you see it."

"Damn you, Charlie. What kind of attempts have been made on you?"

Charlie told him about the hotel-room explosion and the two manmade mechanical problems in the Wagoneer. "I can smell it, Josh," Charlie said. "This is for real."

"Okay," said Josh Bennett.

"I'll be at the Holiday Inn across the road. Please tell nobody, not a soul, not a termite, not a flea, that's where I am. If something happens to me in those last few seconds before I die I'll know it was your fault and I'll come back and haunt you till the day you die. Trust me."

"Trust me, you say," Josh said and stood up. "Up yours, Henderson." He said it in the friendly way they had always exchanged such cracks. But, to Charlie's ear, Josh may have really meant it this time.

Charlie was also now on his feet. "One more thing, please, Josh. You remember Jay Buckner?"

"Yeah. He was a technical-services guy of some kind, wasn't he?"

"Right. See if his life overlays Clark's in any way."

"This could cost me my job, you know, Charlie. You aren't cleared for anything about anything anymore."

"It could prevent the cost of my life, Josh," said Charlie. "You saved it once, how about trying for two?"

They waved as old acquaintances would, having stumbled upon each other accidentally in a large, crowded shopping mall, and left through different entrances.

———————

Charlie's next stop was ten minutes away back in the District just over Chain Bridge, one of seven bridges that crossed the Potomac from the northwest, close to Tyson's Corner to the southeast, several miles past National Airport.

Detective Sergeant Linwood Bock of the Metropolitan D.C. Police had suggested when Charlie called that they meet for "a cup" at a Kentucky Fried Chicken place on MacArthur Boulevard.

Bock was as good at his job as Charlie had suspected.

"The explosive was an East European plastic," he said. "It was strapped to the bottom of the tray with a timer. There was enough to have done some serious damage to a finger or two maybe, but not enough to kill or seriously maim. Somebody doing a little scare job, maybe?"

"Maybe somebody not competent with explosives," Charlie said.

"Nope. This was a pro. It was beautifully placed and arranged. My guess is they wanted only to petrify you, not blow you into the next life. Now, isn't that interesting? Do you know of anybody who would like to scare you but not maim or kill you?"

"I'm still not sure I was the target. There could have been a mistake on the room numbers."

"And I could be chairman of the Michael Dukakis Run Again, Mike, Committee."

Charlie asked about the staff at the hotel.

"The room-service waiter came out clean and we are nowhere with the people in the kitchen or elsewhere in the hotel. Half of them are Ethiopian, the other half are from El Salvador and both kinds hate police and don't remember or know much of anything. The bottom line is that we don't have a line. Not one thing. I can't even find out much about you, Mr. Henderson."

Charlie knew it was coming and he was ready. "There's really not much to know. As I told you, I run a bed-and-breakfast in West Virginia. I worked for the federal government for several years before that."

"You were a spook. I am almost sure of that. Do you wish to confirm or deny?"

"Confirm."

"Thanks. Now, if you had told me that the other day you could have saved me a lot of time and grief."

"I have been out of government for nine years, Sergeant. There is no way what happened to that hotel room could have anything to do with my work. I was a Russian language specialist anyhow. All I did was translate Russian arms and military documents into English." It was a line Charlie had worked out with the Agency to use after his retirement just in case it ever became necessary to admit he had been with the CIA. Every retired operational officer had such a thing arranged in advance in case inquiries did come in that could not be ignored.

It clearly had worked in Bock's case. It was obvious to Charlie that the detective had already been told the Russian language story and Charlie was just confirming it.

"You got any women problems, Mr. Henderson?"

"No, sir. I am sixty-four years old, Sergeant."

"I hope you are not telling me, Mr. Henderson, that life ends at sixty-four."

"I hope I'm not."

"If not women, then what ideas do you have about what could have triggered this kind of thing?"

"I have no idea."

"For the record, Mr. Henderson, let me tell you that I think you are lying through your teeth," Bock said. "But there is not one damned thing I can do about it. All I would say to you is that my experience tells me that citizens who do not wish to cooperate with the police are sometimes citizens who end up without parts of their bodies or even sometimes without even the gift of life itself. Good-bye, sir. My case is closed. I don't know about yours."

═══════════

Back at the Holiday Inn, Charlie called Mike Hanson, the Jefferson County agricultural agent in Charles Town who also owned the HandiMart, a convenience store less than a mile up Highway 51 from Hillmont. He asked Mike for a big favor. The phone at Hillmont was out of order and would he mind going up to the house and asking Mary Jane to come back to the store to the pay phone, where he would call her at six o'clock on the dot? Charlie told Mike: "Tell her to remember Operation Joplin Jaguar." Mike said he would be glad to deliver the message.

And at six o'clock Charlie dialed the number of the HandiMart's pay phone. Mary Jane picked it up before the first ring got a decent start.

"This is the Nantucket Bucket," she said. "Who is this?"

"The Joplin Jaguar," Charlie said back.

It was not one of those cutesy little jokes between married couples. It came out of a terrifying experience they had had in Tunis right before Charlie retired. They had gone there on a side trip after two weeks in Italy to spend a few days of unofficial vacation with Jack Donnelly, the United States ambassador to Tunisia, and his wife, Marge. They had known each other for twenty years, from when Charlie and Jack served in the United States embassy in Cairo together. Jack had been the real political attaché; Charlie was under the cover of being an economics attaché. In Tunis Mary Jane and Marge had gone out for a shopping trip into the medina in the old-town part of Tunis, a maze of narrow pedestrian streets that dated back to the twelfth century and were now full of stalls run by aggressive peddlers of pottery, jewelry, rugs and other goods. Inside one of the rug stalls a young Tunisian invited them to follow him through a door into a room where even more and cheaper rugs were kept. A Tunisian who worked for the United States embassy as a driver/bodyguard stepped forward to accompany them, but out of the shadows came several men who pushed him aside and the two women on through the door. Marge and Mary Jane were quickly blindfolded and tied to chairs. And before long they were confronted by somebody who said he was a Palestinian who wanted to trade some information to Israel about a terrorist group in exchange for getting his wife and two children safely out of Lebanon. A deal was in fact finally struck, but before it was all over Mary Jane and Charlie had a series of phone conversations in which they used "Joplin Jaguar" and "Nantucket Bucket" to establish bona fides.

"Assume for a while that somebody is listening to what is said on our phone at Hillmont," Charlie now said to Mary Jane at the HandiMart. "I will call the house occasionally but assume everything I tell you is bullshit. If I have something real to say I will do as we did in Tunis. I will call, let it ring twice and then hang up. Then again in two minutes with three rings. Exactly seventeen minutes later I will call this number at the HandiMart."

Charlie waited for Mary Jane to say something. She didn't. So he said, "Are there any questions?"

"Oh, no, not a one. Why would I have any questions? Isn't this normal behavior for sixty-four-year-old men?"

"Trust me."

"Good-bye, Charlie. I will listen for your rings."

Tourists and others not in the know called it the National Cathedral, but the real official name of that magnificent Episcopal cathedral at the corner of Wisconsin and Massachusetts avenues was the Washington Cathedral. The "National" label was understandable because it was where presidents of the United States came for inaugural religious services, where the most prominent of the nation's leaders were memorialized at death and where major peace vigils and similar events occurred, usually on national television. What only a few people knew was that it was also a center of Washington's very active spy industry. Intelligence officers of all nations and stripes met, whispered, exchanged goodies, dead-dropped messages and did other spylike things in and around the cathedral. There were several reasons for it, the most important being simply one of location. Three blocks south on Wisconsin was the Soviet embassy's residence compound. Down Massachusetts in easy walking distance were the British, South African, Danish, Brazilian, Canadian and Norwegian embassies. The Belgians and the Japanese were also close by, as had been the Iranians before their embassy was closed and confiscated by the United States government. In Charlie's time, the CIA had two safe houses within five blocks of the cathedral, and he was told the FBI had three.

Another reason for the cathedral's use was its sheer size and design. It was a rabbit warren of hallways and small alcoves and chapels and other places that made it easy for an individual to appear nonchalant and one of many. Most everyone but the spies came to ooh and ah over the gorgeous stained-glass windows, the statues of Washington and Lincoln in the back, the beautifully embroidered prayer cushions and all the rest. Few people came to watch what other people were doing.

So it came as no surprise to Charlie that Josh suggested they meet that evening at eight-thirty in the Chapel of the Good Shepherd. He didn't even have to say the Washington Cathedral because Josh knew that Charlie would know what he meant.

The Good Shepherd was the smallest of the chapels and the only one that was open for private prayer twenty-four hours a day. The entrance was down an outside hallway on the north side of the cathedral, so it was not necessary to go into the sanctuary or anywhere else in the main building to get to it. It was not much larger than a closet, was neither heated nor air-conditioned and had no removable parts, only two small pews bolted to the floor that seated two people each and a third that had room for only one. The walls were all gray granite, as was a wall sculpture of a shepherd holding a lamb that was up front over a small marble table that functioned as a kind of altar.

Josh was already there, sitting in one of the two-person pews. Charlie sat down in the single one across a tiny aisle on the left.

"Like old times," Charlie said. "It was in here that the Purple Poet started spilling his guts."

"Churkinoff also," Josh said.

"The Purple Poet" was the inside code name for a distinguished Palestinian-American poet and literary critic who taught nine-teenth-century English literature at Georgetown University. He served on the PLO's Palestine National Council, the international group that considered itself a Palestinian government of sorts in exile, but for his own internal Palestinian political reasons he hated Yasir Arafat. So he told the Agency everything he knew and could find out about Arafat. Churkinoff was a young second secretary at the Soviet embassy who had originally been turned by the CIA when he was stationed in Paris. He sang and handed over microfilmed documents for money that he said he needed to open his own Russian restaurant on the Left Bank someday when he got tired of diplomacy. No cash ever changed hands at the Chapel of the Good Shepherd or anywhere else because he had the Agency put his money directly into a bank account in Geneva.

"I looked at everything we had on Clark," Josh said, his voice a practiced flat monotone that was audible only to someone sitting exactly where Charlie was. "Nothing leaps out. He got high marks from every supervisor in every assignment. He worked inside and outside. Just about every fitness report said something about his brilliance, diligence and all of that other crap. He ran a string of assets in Spain, another in Lisbon before the revolution. No scars in any of that. He was on a brief special assignment for a while after the Kennedy assassination but presumably so were a lot of people. There were no details of that."

Charlie said, "What about Buckner?"

"There were several matches, several times they worked together. Buckner was in Lisbon with Clark and they were in Paris at the same time."

"Were they tight?"

"Tightness is not on the fitness form, Charlie. I do not know. But I would doubt it. As you know, tech-services people are looked upon as clod plumbers by high fliers like Clark . . . and you."

"Anything from CI?"

CI was counterintelligence, the search for moles and other security leaks within the Agency and its operations.

"He passed every flutter with no problems." Flutter was the term for being tested on the polygraph, commonly known as the lie detector. It was a joke inside the Agency because most everyone including Charlie knew a method using Valium or something to beat it. "Angleton got onto him once but there was nothing there."

"What was that all about?"

"There wasn't anything to it. Angleton was trying to tie him into the Blunt-Philby crowd at Cambridge, something like that. Angleton figured everybody who was even in the world at the time was suspect."

Angleton was James Jesus Angleton, the famous CIA counterintelligence chief. He became famous because he wrote poetry, grew orchids, ate lunch most days at the same French restaurant in Washington and suspected various CIA directors and other high officials of being Soviet moles. He died in 1987 after being embarrassed by the Church Committee for running the infamous Cointel program that opened people's mail and infiltrated various leftwing organizations, among other things. He was one of those rare people about which the legends were mostly true or understated. No book about the Agency, pro or con, has ever left him out or alone. Charlie had also read a novel that was based on Angleton called *Orchids for Mother.* "Mother" was one of Angleton's in-house nicknames.

"Nothing at all came of it?" Charlie asked.

"Nope, per usual with Angleton's stuff."

"Who besides Angleton in CI worked on the case?"

"I think it was Reynolds. Clay Reynolds. But forget it, Charlie. You know how Angleton was."

Yes, indeed. Charlie knew exactly how Angleton was. Which was sometimes crazy but not always.

"Thanks for this, Josh," Charlie said.

"Thanks for what?"

"For risking your important job to save my unimportant life."

Their meeting was over. Charlie was the first to stand.

"What's going on, Charlie?" Josh asked as he got up.

"Can't say yet," Charlie said.

"Did you know about Bruce Conn Clark's Blue Heart, by the way?" Josh said.

Charlie shook his head.

"He and Buckner were in a scrape together in Lisbon in '62. Some Bulgarian thug put a bullet in Clark's right shoulder. He left the Agency shortly afterward."

It was only after he had driven away from the cathedral that Charlie realized he had just done something very stupid, something that showed there was still much more rust to come off. In the world of Washington, spooks going to the Washington Cathedral was like going to Grand Central Station. Or at least it could be. Or at least he should have thought of that when Josh suggested it.

He was four blocks south on Wisconsin in front of the Soviet compound coming up to the intersection with Calvert Avenue. Instead of going straight he took a right fork on Thirty-fifth Street across Calvert and quickly stopped at a parking meter and turned off the car lights. Nobody came whizzing by. He saw or felt nothing wrong.

Then he remembered Germaine's, a Vietnamese restaurant in the next block that a lot of news and other public people went to. So did a lot of private-intelligence types. There were several restaurants in the area that at any given time in Charlie's pre-*glasnost* days were full of assorted agents.

Germaine, a Vietnamese woman married to a news photographer she met in Vietnam during the war, greeted him warmly, as she did everyone. There was no reason for her to remember him, but she, like Lucy DeCarlo, acted as if she did. She also honored his request for a table in the back room. He sat so that he could watch the front entrance and feasted on two spring rolls, lemon chicken and rice plus a bottle of Tsing-Tao beer.

He felt bad about Josh. But there was simply no way he could tell him everything. Not now. Not until he knew himself what was happening. And maybe not even then. His other thought about Josh was simply that Josh was no fool. If he put his splendid mind and his access to Agency records to it he might even figure some of it out for himself.

So much for thinking.

Charlie felt satisfaction with a good meal and even a bit with himself when he left Germaine's almost ninety minutes later. But, just in case, instead of going directly back to the Holiday Inn he went north for a while and then back across to Massachusetts, through downtown, across the Fourteenth Street bridge to National Airport and to Budget's twenty-four-hour facility. There he turned in his Plymouth Fury for a cream-colored Chevy van.

The game. It felt good to be playing again.

———

Charlie made only one call before going to sleep in one of the two double beds in his Holiday Inn room. It was to Hillmont.

"Well, I got here," he said to Mary Jane. "Philadelphia's never looked better."

"Give my best to everyone," Mary Jane said.

"I will. Particularly to Bill and Helene. How are our guests?"

"All is well."

"Tell them I am sorry that I am not there to play host in my tweeds."

"I will," said Mary Jane. "I will."

"Save me some of those Martha Washington chicken patties."

"I'll do it."

"Good night and I love you," said Charlie.

"Same to you and double the bid," said Mary Jane, the ever-reliable Nantucket Bucket.

———

The next day, Sunday, was a wasted day for Charlie. He spent it in his motel room reading the *Post* and *The New York Times* and watching television. Staying completely out of sight for twenty-four hours or more was a recognized and necessary tool of his old trade. Many an intelligence transaction had been blown because somebody did not have the patience and the self-discipline it takes to remain stationary, silent, out of sight.

And this twenty-four hours wasn't a complete bust. Bruce Conn Clark, in what Lesley Stahl said was a "last-minute change," was on CBS's *Face the Nation*. He and Henry Kissinger debated the wisdom of using force to get Saddam Hussein and Iraq out of Kuwait. Clark was in favor of giving economic and political sanctions more time to work, Kissinger was not. Charlie, who was not sure what he thought about it himself, enjoyed the exchange. Since his retirement, he had gradually lost his interest in such matters as war and peace. Iraq invades Kuwait. So what? It didn't have anything to do with Charlie. Not anymore.

Charlie laughed out loud at himself when he realized he had been lying in his bed listening without much passion to these two brilliant minds go at it. Never mind that one of them, the smooth guy without the accent there on Lesley Stahl's left, was apparently out to kill, maim or scare him.

I have a question, Miss Stahl! I have a question for Mr. Bruce Conn Clark!

Ask it, Mr. Henderson.

Mr. Bruce Conn Clark, are you trying to kill, maim or scare Mr. Charles Avenue Henderson? And whichever, why?

═══════════

Finding Clay Reynolds, the former CI man, led Charlie's Monday morning agenda.

There was a guy in McLean who kept a roster of former intelligence agents for an organization that David Phillips started after the Church Committee investigations. Phillips had been a high-level Agency man in Latin America. He was incensed at how intelligence officers and the intelligence profession were being beat up on, so he set up a group to "tell the other side." He and other former agents appeared on television programs and did newspaper and print interviews in an attempt to convince the American people that CIA agents were not all assassins who put explosives in the beards of the Fidel Castros of this world. Charlie was still in the Agency at the time so he appreciated what Phillips did. Others, like Josh, thought the whole thing was stupid because it violated the number-one rule of the business—no-profile secrecy.

The McLean man said he had no record of Reynolds. "CI people, mostly, don't join our things because they assume we, like all other American organizations and institutions, have been infiltrated by the Russians, the Chinese, the Iranians, the Sandinistas, the PLO, the Greens, the Democratic party, the PTA and all other enemies of the American Way of Life," he explained. But he did give Charlie the name of a woman who lived in Chevy Chase, a namey section of northwest Washington that had parts in both the District and Maryland. He said she had been one of Angleton's top assistants and had retired at the same time that Angleton was forced out. She might know something about Reynolds.

The woman's name was Angela Eakin. She lived in an expensive luxury apartment house just west of the upscale Chevy Chase shopping area. She agreed to see him only after she did something to check him out. Charlie had no idea of whom she might have called to see if he was all right. And he also had no idea of what her idea of all right might be.

Charlie would never have picked her out of a lineup. Tall, thin, together, seventy, designer-dressed, traveled, degree-ed, she was not a normal CI type, although he realized as he thought it that few of any kinds of people are. She also either married or inherited a lot of money. Retired career Agency people did not live quite this well, this way.

"Why do you want to know about Reynolds?" she said after only a few minutes of preliminaries. "Please tell me everything and tell me straight the first time around, Mr. Henderson. We both have enough in common to know that there are two ways to do these kinds of things, the fast way and the slow way. I have only time for and interest in the fast way. I know from my inquiries that you were very good at what you did for the Agency, but I also know that what you are doing now, whatever it is, is not official. At least, those who repute to know say it is not. I would be among the first to admit, however, that one cannot always be sure of that kind of thing no matter who tells you. I knew of you at the Agency, of course, and it is unfortunate that our paths did not cross while we were there, but considering each of our specialities that is not unusual."

True. The people involved in looking for moles and leaks did not hang around with anybody except their own kind, and that was the same for the covert-operations people like Charlie. Angela Eakin knew of Charlie because CI checked out everybody. And that meant everybody.

Charlie liked the way she talked. She had an accent he decided was Colorado. Or possibly northern New Mexico or Wyoming. All of her sophistication and experience could not hide that, and a great thing about her was that she did not seem to care.

Charlie had only a breath or two to decide how to play this thing with Angela Eakin. Here, as with Bruce, were two old warriors sparring like it was old times, like it mattered. For Charlie, of course, it mattered very much. He was in Bruce Conn Clark's cross hairs for reasons he did not understand.

"It's about Bruce Conn Clark," said Charlie, having decided he had nothing to lose by going the fast, straight way. "As you may know he worked for the Agency in the sixties. As you may also know he was the subject of a CI investigation at one time. I want to know the nature of that investigation."

"Why?"

"Because I have reason to believe it might relate to something he is trying to do to me now."

"What is he trying to do to you?"

"Kill me."

"Would you like a cup of coffee?" said Angela Eakin. "Or some tea. We have all kinds, decaffeinated as well as the other."

He said he would love a cup of straight coffee and she disappeared. Smart lady, thought Charlie. She's buying some time to think about it. Smart me for taking her up on the coffee and thus giving her that time. He seldom drank coffee anymore because it kept him awake and he hated decaffeinated because it didn't keep him awake.

Angela Eakin's apartment was everything Charlie hated in rich people's places to live. The rugs were too thick, the chairs too stuffed, the mirrors too big, the picture frames too silver, the colors too beige. One of the best things about Hillmont was that he and Mary Jane had kept rugs off the natural-wood floors and furniture to a minimum.

She returned with the coffee. She had a small white porcelain teapot for herself. She poured herself a cup and said: "What is the connection between a CI investigation of Clark in the sixties and his interest in killing you now?"

"There may not be any. I'm trying to find out if there is."

She took a long sip of her tea. "The investigation had to do with his brother, not Clark himself," she said. Her accent was still there but now she was giving a report. "His brother, I think his name was Ralph, had been a student at Cambridge at the same time as Guy Burgess, Blunt and the other colorful young Marxists. Mr. Angleton thought that was worth exploring. So it was explored."

"What was the conclusion?"

"There was no conclusion. With Mr. Angleton cases were never concluded because he took the position that nothing was ever really finally everlastingly provable and thus everlastingly closeable and concludeable. All I know is that nothing ever happened, no action was ever recommended or taken. Reynolds, if I remember correctly, interviewed a few people, but as I recall he found out nothing incriminating about Bruce Conn Clark. And that, after all, was the purpose of the investigation."

"Was Clark fluttered?"

"I'm sure he was. But I am sure he passed with flying colors or sirens and bells would have gone off all over CI."

Charlie took a swallow of coffee. "Where could I find Clay Reynolds?" he asked.

"Right here."

"What?"

"Clay and I married right after I left the Agency. He had left years before to enter the insurance business and was then divorced. I was a widow. Mr. Angleton believed in closeness among the people of CI. He discouraged friends outside CI, and Clay and I followed orders."

"Well, I don't know what to say," Charlie said, proving his point that he did not know what to say.

"People who don't do their homework seldom do, Mr. Henderson," she said.

It occurred to Charlie that Angela Eakin might have been more than Jim Angleton's assistant. She might have also been his twin sister.

———————

Charlie had parked his Chevy van around the corner from the apartment on a side street that two blocks west came out in an upscale shopping area that included Brooks Brothers. He had been a dress-shirt freak in the old days, there being few things he loved more than going into a place like Brooks Brothers on impulse and buying two or three shirts. It led to a time back when he was traveling so often on short notice that he had fifty-four dress shirts. He knew the exact number because Mary Jane counted them one day.

The twitch hit him again. So he walked right on past the van to Brooks Brothers. A young woman who didn't seem to care if he shopped there or not showed him an array of 17½-35 shirts. Most of them were stripes with button-down collars, which was fine with

Charlie. He chose a dark blue stripe and put it on his American Express card. The whole process made him feel good and young. And rust-free.

━━━━━━━

The one lesson all intelligence officers learn early is the value of local public libraries. Newspapers on microfilm, little magazines, telephone and city directories from all over, and books about obscure subjects can be most helpful to the traveling agent in need of information in a hurry. So that was why Charlie went from Brooks Brothers to the Montgomery County branch library on Arlington Boulevard in Bethesda. In less than five minutes he was looking at a microfilm copy of the 1975 Sunday *New York Times Magazine* profile of Bruce Conn Clark by William Safire. Way down in it was the line he was looking for: "Mr. Clark was born in Ithaca, New York, the youngest of three sons. The oldest, Duane Rollins Clark, became an academic. He recently retired after 35 years as a professor of art history at Vassar College in Poughkeepsie, New York."

From a pay phone in the library's lobby he called the art-history department at Vassar. Professor Clark, he was told, now lived on Kiawah Island, a South Carolina resort south of Charleston.

While he was there he called Mary Jane again at Hillmont.

"Bad news, sweetheart," said the Joplin Jaguar. "This awful truck of ours has thrown a clutch."

"Where did it throw it?" said the Nantucket Bucket.

"All over itself. It means spending the night—maybe even a good part of tomorrow—here."

"Where's here?"

"Lancaster, Pennsylvania. I couldn't get in the Howard Johnson's so I don't know where I'll be staying."

"Watch out for the Amish horse-and-buggies."

"Will do."

"Ring me anytime."

And they said good-bye. He knew what she meant by saying "ring" but decided to ignore it for now. Maybe later in the day he would set up a real call at the HandiMart.

Right now he had to think about Duane Rollins Clark.

He went back into the library's reference department. There was no listing for Duane Rollins Clark in any of the *Who's Who* or other biographical books. He went to the art section, which was a combination of coffee-table books about famous artists and their work and scholarly studies of various schools of art. There were nearly forty books on the shelves, and none of them, he saw very quickly, was written by Clark. Now what? He decided to just start looking through them. Maybe he would see something that struck a chord. Charlie was no expert on art but he did know the major names and periods—enough to make the job at least interesting.

As it turned out, it was his knowledge of his own trade that did it. After twenty minutes of skim searching he had in his hand a book by Sir Anthony Blunt about fourteenth-century Renaissance paintings. Blunt was the late art adviser to the queen of England and was the famous Fourth Man in the Soviet espionage ring with Burgess, Maclean and Philby that started at Cambridge. Charlie turned to the acknowledgments page. And there he read the following sentence:

"I want to thank also my longtime friend and fellow art historian Duane Rollins Clark of Vassar College, Poughkeepsie, New York, U.S.A."

———

There was somebody in a dark blue Mercury sedan in the parking lot at the Holiday Inn directly across from Charlie's first-floor room. Charlie saw him before he saw Charlie because of the van. Clearly the guy was on the lookout for something else. A green Plymouth Fury, maybe? Charlie swung the van away from the parking-lot entrance at the last minute and went around the other side of the two-story building. He stopped the van in the back and got scared and felt very old and outgunned. Clearly he was up against some top people with access to just about everything anyone on a hunt to kill would ever need. Including maybe even the number-two man in the CIA. Only Josh knew he was staying there. Could Josh have a connection to Bruce Conn Clark? Clark had been secretary of state after all. The only other way anybody could have found out would have been through various kinds of exotic surveillance—electronic or otherwise. He suddenly wondered if somebody had put a new kind of homing device on him that had been invented after he retired. Or were all Holiday Inn people paid to be on the lookout for him? The simplest and most logical explanation, of course, was Angela Eakin. She had not only agreed to see him but also passed on that fact to somebody tied in with Bruce Conn Clark. And he had been tailed ever since he left her apartment. But he was pretty good at picking up a tail and he had not seen a thing. Of course, there may be some new high-tech way to tail cars as well.

Now what?

It was a question he never had to answer. Because a young man in a suit had come up on his blind side and was standing there by the front door of the van. It was at that split second that Charlie also came to grips with the fact that he was completely defenseless. He had no firearm, not even a pocketknife. He was an old man who should have stayed walking the tracks in West Virginia and figured out another way to deal with the problem of Bruce Conn Clark.

He thought about Hillmont and the wildflowers and cattails in the wetlands. He thought about Mary Jane and what a problem arranging the funeral would be. At least she knew where to bury him. He had written all that down thirty-five years ago. The plot was waiting for him at Memorial Park in Joplin next to his mother and father.

And the only thing that would be said about him at that funeral and in the *Post*'s obituary was that Charles Avenue Henderson had been an intelligence officer for the Central Intelligence Agency. There would be no details, no mention of the special Kennedy assassination assignment or anything else, including his Blue Heart.

The young man motioned for Charlie to roll down his window. So Charlie did. Go in quiet and in peace, Henderson.

"Mr. Henderson?" said the young man.

Charlie said nothing.

The young man said: "Mr. Bennett is waiting for you in that car around on the other side. He would like to talk to you."

Josh! It was Josh Bennett in that dark Mercury. Oh, thank you, you wonderful God.

"You deserve to die, Charlie," said Josh. "If Clark doesn't get you, maybe I will."

"Sorry," Charlie mumbled. He was still glowing with relief that the man in the car was not a Clark killer. He could feel a little anger in Josh but he knew it was the kind that would pass, the kind flavored with concern for a friend.

They were walking out in the open down toward the end of the parking lot. They agreed with their eyes that talking inside Charlie's room might not be a wise thing to do.

"Let me tell you what I did, Charlie. I left the cathedral intrigued by the fact that you didn't respond when I said Clark worked on the Kennedy assassination investigation." Josh was taking his time, as Charlie remembered he often did when making a report. Charlie remembered that he was always accused, even by his friends in the Agency, of "burying the lead." And of being boring.

In this case Charlie did not mind. The longer Josh took to get it out, the longer it gave him to decide how to react. He knew what was coming.

"There was no paper around where it should have been. None of those little blue and yellow sheets that summarize the work done by Intelligence Officer A-6, say, and Intelligence Officer B-14, say. Not a scrap. Now, I found that strange because if there is one thing that we do, Charlie, it is to keep things that our people write down on paper about what they do. The exceptions, of course, are things that we decide never happened or things that are so special and super top secret that they end up in special places that only a very privileged few know about. So I thought about it awhile and then I said, Wait a minute, I am the deputy director of this agency and that makes me one of the privileged few. So I resumed my search in other places. And, lo and behold, I found some yellow and blue pieces of paper. I found some that said Intelligence Officer A-6, of all people, and Intelligence Officer B-14, of all people, had been given a special, most sensitive joint assignment. I did a little bit of cross-checking and discovered that Intelligence Officer A-6 was none other than Bruce Conn Clark and Intelligence Officer B-14 was none other than Charles Avenue Henderson. When we have a moment over a malted milk sometime I would like you to tell me again how in the hell you got that middle name Avenue, by the way. I know you have told me before but I have forgotten . . ."

"My mother was driven by a sense of place. She was born on Charles Avenue in Sedalia, Missouri, so why not commemorate that fact by so naming her first-born son."

"I said that could wait for another time, Charlie. The special, most sensitive assignment was given to them on the evening of November 22, 1963. It was given to them personally by the director of Central Intelligence on orders from the newly sworn-in president of the United States. That must have been some assignment, Charlie."

"Yeah, you might say that," Charlie said. They were now walking very slowly around the parking lot. "What else did your little papers say?"

"That's pretty much where it ends," Josh said. "There are all kinds of official notations around about you and Clark being sent back to your regular assignments afterward. But I could not find any piece of paper that said what you did. I guess that never got written down?"

Josh waited a few seconds. "That was a question, Charlie."

"I know. The answer is that I do not remember anything being written down by us. Our report was an oral report."

More silence.

"Okay, Charlie," Josh said. "What about the report?"

"I don't want to say anything about that now," Charlie said.

"I'm tired of walking around," Josh said. "Let's go sit in my car."

"Let's go sit in my van, if you don't mind."

"Trust with you only goes one way, doesn't it?" Josh was hot. "I am not going to wire you or bug you or videotape you or do anything else to you, for God's sake! I'm just tired of walking around this goddamn parking lot!"

"Hey, hey. You are still an official of the U.S. government. You have taken oaths to uphold all kinds of things. I do not want to put you in a position to have to choose between your official duties and my neck."

Josh shrugged. And they walked over and got into the cream Chevy van, Charlie behind the wheel, Josh in the passenger's seat. The young man who had come with Josh was still around somewhere, obviously, Charlie knew, as were probably other young men from Security.

"Did something happen in November 1963 that makes Bruce Conn Clark want to kill you now?" Josh said once they were settled.

"I do not know for sure myself. That's what I'm trying to find out."

"Tell me what you do know."

"No," Charlie said.

" 'No.' You ask my help and then you tell me nothing. Why didn't you tell me about this assassination thing? You knew from the beginning it had to do with that. This is not the way to operate with me, Charlie."

"Josh, there's something involved in this that . . . well, I felt I simply could not, cannot, tell you. Not now. Not yet. I gave my word."

"To whom?"

"Clark."

"The sonofabitch is trying to kill you!"

"Maybe it's not that simple."

"Don't use that word again."

"What word?"

"Simple."

They sat in silence for several seconds, both of them looking ahead or out their own side of the van.

"You're going to have to take him on directly," Josh said.

"Clark?"

"Clark."

"Great idea, Mr. Deputy Director. I will go out and assemble my own army of former technical-services bombers and killers like Buckner, and he will do the same, and we can have a shootout at RFK Stadium or something. Maybe at halftime during a Redskins game."

Josh looked over at Charlie. "You're an old fart with a good chance of having his balls and his life blown off at any second but you haven't lost your sense of humor. Good for you, Charlie." He looked back straight. "I mean go to him and confront him. Not with an AK-47 or a plastic bomb, but just demand to know what in the hell is going on. You can't go on like this, Charlie. One or two things are going to happen otherwise and one of them is you die."

"Talk about simple," Charlie said.

"No offense, Charles Avenue, but you are sixty-four years old, you are in no position to spend the rest of your life dodging bombs and cut fuel lines."

"I know that, thank you."

They fell silent again, which was no problem. Real friends have no problem with silence. Charlie knew Josh was right about the reality of the situation. Buying a shirt at Brooks Brothers and playing Joplin Jaguar and shaking tails and all the rest did not bring him back to real life as a warrior. And he thought about Josh's simple idea. It didn't take long for him to figure out that he didn't have a better one. At least right now. At least yet. There was still time to think, though. He still had time. Clark and his people hopefully were looking in Lancaster, Pennsylvania. He would call Mary Jane again soon and say he was somewhere else. Maybe something had come up in Pittsburgh. Right. He would be on his way to Pittsburgh.

Clark's brother must be the key. Yes, indeed. The brother, the retired art professor in South Carolina. He's it.

Josh said after a while, "Good luck, Charlie."

Charlie grunted something. His mind was already wondering if it was USAir or Delta that flew to Charleston, South Carolina.

PART
TWO

Bruce

October 7–14, 1990

DeCarlo's was not on Bruce's normal rounds. He had given up thick Italian sauces and wines when he was shuttling around the world on behalf of the United States of America. Flying overnight to Riyadh for a meeting with a king and then on to Amman for a meeting with another king and then back to England and France for meetings with premiers and prime ministers does not mix with heavy food and drink. It was bad for the mind as well as the waistline. And by the time he left government and the pressure was off, the habit of careful wining and dining was there to stay.

But the Xerox executives had said DeCarlo's, so DeCarlo's it would be. He got out of the car and had trouble remembering if he had even been there before. One of the problems with having done as much as he had in his life was that he could not remember it all. People who do little have trouble understanding that simple fact of life and often get offended when the Bruce Conn Clarks do not remember meeting them at a World Affairs dinner in Los

Angeles, at a cocktail party at the Council of Foreign Relations in New York, on a Concorde flight to London.

"May I help you, sir?" said an attractive woman at the door.

Clark was genuinely stunned that the person in charge of this restaurant did not immediately recognize him. It had been a while since Bruce had been to a restaurant anywhere in the world where he was not expected or recognized and thus fussed over.

"My name is Bruce Conn Clark," said Bruce to Lucy DeCarlo. "I am here to meet a Mr. Howard Adams."

"Oh, yes, sir," said Lucy DeCarlo. "Of course, Mr. Secretary. It is an honor having you in our restaurant. Welcome, sir. If you will come right this way. Your table is ready. Mr. Adams is already here."

So she knows the name but not the face, thought Bruce. At least all is not lost.

The Xerox men wanted some advice from Bruce on how to handle a sticky problem with China. A Xerox sales representative in Beijing had been caught consorting with a dissident political leader. The sales guy, an American born to Chinese parents, said he was only trying to peddle copiers and other products to the dissident movement. The Chinese government accused him of antigovernment behavior and threw the man in jail. Lawyers there and in the United States told Xerox to expect a show trial and a sentence of up to twenty years.

Bruce listened and commiserated and was concluding a long statement about the difficulty in securing a political solution to the problem when he saw a man enter the back room of the restaurant who looked vaguely familiar, a common experience for Bruce.

Bruce smiled at the man, which was a mistake. The man then started toward Bruce's table.

Damn it, who is this guy?

"Secretary Clark, I'm Charlie Henderson."

It still didn't register.

"November 1963."

Charlie Henderson. Oh, yes. Oh, yes! Charlie Henderson! A few deep breaths and dark memory flashes later, he remembered him. He was on the list. This man out of the past was one the few people in the world who had the power to absolutely destroy Bruce Conn Clark. There were others, but Bruce did not know exactly how many or most of their names. Bruce had hoped and prayed that he might live out his life before one of them did something.

It was not to be.

Here was this man Charlie Henderson talking about old secrets.

Charlie Henderson, standing here now in front of him. Charlie Henderson, like Bruce, had taken good care of himself. Good skin color, no stomach. There was even some hair left on the top of this man's head, as there was on his.

Here was this man Charlie Henderson talking about old secrets.

———————

Once he had decided what to do, Bruce wasted no time. He did not even think twice about the black-tie dinner commitment he already had at Meridian House four nights later. Meridian House was a mansion off Sixteenth Street north of downtown that had been the family home of the Meyers, the *Washington Post* family. Now it housed an international-affairs center. Bruce was to give a toast in honor of the Danish ambassador and his wife, who were moving on to a new assignment back in Copenhagen. He merely had his assistant, a young man named Kermit Cushing, call the Meridian House people to cancel. He gave Cushing no reason for the cancellation. When you were Bruce Conn Clark you never had to give reasons.

His reason was a meeting with Jay Buckner.

———————

Jay seemed disappointed. "I never figured Charlie for blackmail. He must be hard up for money, which I do not understand. He paid cash for that old house, you know. Maybe it's his wife's money."

Jay was sitting on one of two huge leather couches in Bruce's private office, which resembled a museum of the life and accomplishments of Bruce Conn Clark. One whole wall was covered with expensively framed eight-by-ten black-and-white photographs of Bruce with just about everybody who had ever been anybody in any part of the world in the last thirty years. Prime ministers Wilson, Callaghan and Thatcher; Trudeau, Clark and Mulroney. Kings Hassan, Hussein, Orlof and Juan Carlos. Queens Elizabeth and Beatrix. Chancellors Adenauer, Brandt, Schmidt and Kohl. Emperor Hirohito. Presidents Giscard d'Estaing, Mitterand, De Klerk, Johnson, Nixon, Ford, Carter, Reagan and Bush, plus all kinds of vice-presidents, speakers, majority and minority leaders, whips, industrialists, entertainers, novelists, athletes, Billy Grahams and like men of God. All were inscribed to Bruce with words of respect and admiration.

There were also things standing and lying about, such as the seal and flag of the secretary of state, ashtrays, letter openers, desk pen-and-pencil sets and clocks that were engraved with special citations, messages or emblems of historical importance.

"I take it you are not going to tell somebody as lowlife as me why he is blackmailing you." Jay said.

"You got it, Jaybird," said Bruce.

Buckner was, like Charlie and Bruce, a man in his sixties. His relationship with Bruce Conn Clark was one that stuck despite their having lived very different lives and gone their very separate ways after they worked together at the Agency. They were easy together because of what they had been through together as young men, not because they were alike or because they were friends. All they shared were experiences, which were the most adhesive of the bonds between men, particularly if those experiences were in the military, sports or spying.

"So what, then, Your Majesty, are my orders?" Jay asked.

"Scare him," said Bruce. "Scare him into thinking he is going to die."

"Is he?"

"Is he what?"

"Going to die?"

"No."

"Should he know who is doing it?" Jay asked.

"Not yet," Bruce said.

Buckner, also like Charlie and Bruce, was still physically together. He was about six feet tall, weighed over two hundred pounds, most of which was well distributed and fairly tight, except for a few pounds that gathered in a small ball over his belt.

"I could be rusty, you know," said Buckner. "There's a fine line between scaring somebody good and killing them for good. So what happens if something goes slightly wrong and Charlie's history?"

Bruce Conn Clark stood, turned both of his hands palms upward and said: "I would speak eloquently at the funeral."

"You are still a bastard, Brucebear," Buckner said. You don't know the half of it, Jaybird, thought Brucebear.

"I do not deny that," Bruce said. "But I would very much hate it if Charlie Henderson died. He does not deserve that just for trying a little blackmail. He really doesn't. So please, try very hard to only scare. I am very serious about that."

"I hear you," said Jay Buckner.

———————

Bruce awoke a few mornings later at six-thirty to the voices of WTOP's all-news radio. He listened quietly but fully awake to the summary of the overnight local news. There was nothing on it that sounded like it was the work of Jaybird. Bruce knew it was too early according to the plan, but he also knew plans do not always work. It was even possible that Charlie Henderson had not come to the Brookings affair as planned.

He got up and fixed his regular breakfast of a muffin, grapefruit juice and decaf coffee. The muffins were made especially for him by a woman in Bethesda who was the sister of a secretary in his office. She used some kind of special recipe to make muffins that were free of cholesterol and polyunsaturated fat, contained only 178 calories, but were large, moist and filling. She made them in a wide variety of flavors that included pumpkin yogurt, orange walnut and cherry chocolate, as well as the standard blueberry, oat bran and raisin. Every Sunday evening the woman dropped off a bag of a mixed dozen of the muffins individually wrapped in cellophane at the front desk of Watergate West, Bruce's building.

Bruce Conn Clark lived alone, and both of his ex-wives would probably have argued that he always had. Even when he was married. Wife One, the former Madge Cronin, was now the present Madge Cronin Morris, the wife of an American Express vice-president, and lived in Nyack, New York. She and Bruce had been one of those classic Northeast good-families couples who came together because of where they came from and where they went to school. They met when she was a sophomore at Wellesley and he was a junior at Harvard. Madge, after first being fascinated, came to hate everything about Bruce's being in the CIA, particularly his not telling her what he was doing and where he was going. Shortly after their sixth wedding anniversary, which he had missed, he came home from Berlin to their empty Washington apartment in Sedgwick Gardens on Connecticut Avenue. She was gone forever. They had had no children, so the official parting was quick, painless and polite.

That was not true in the case of Wife Two, even though there were also no children. Bruce and the former Sharon Leah Runyan grew to hate each other before they parted after only four years of marriage. Bruce was the president's national security adviser and Sharon was a brilliant young economist on the staff of the National

Security Council when they met and married in a courtship that drew a lot of cooing publicity. She specialized in sifting through and synthesizing CIA and other analyses of the frailty of other nation's economies, particularly in the hot areas like the Middle East. When Bruce was named secretary of state he did not take her with him to the State Department, a move he felt would be misunderstood by the press and the public as well as the president. Bruce prospered and shone on the international stage; she stayed very much at the low level and out of all spotlights except his. And after a while she accused Bruce of intentionally keeping her there professionally, a charge that outraged him. There were awful scenes on airplanes, in the backseats of limos, in their Watergate bedroom, in four-star hotel suites and all kinds of other places. She was now a professor of international economics at Stanford University, happily married to an Australian-born professor of linguistics at the University of California at Berkeley.

Bruce had since had a series of female friends and companions, but no wives, no live-ins. In the last few years he had found the need lessened but the desire heightened, or maybe the other way around.

This morning, as he dressed, he felt strangely envious of Charlie Henderson. How many kids did Charlie have? At least three, probably. And grandchildren? At least eight, probably. Bruce was not often envious. He had not often been able to see himself as a father or grandfather except at Christmastime, which he usually spent with his childless brother in Poughkeepsie or South Carolina or with old friends at Middleburg, and on his own birthdays. He thought it would be terrific to have a lot of children and grandchildren around then, singing songs and telling stories and giving him gifts and kisses and hugs. Oh, well. One has to make decisions and then live with them without whining.

He had always believed that as long as you were in charge of your own life, as long as you decided what you were and what you did, the fall of the resulting chips was irrelevant.

He had always believed that. But not this time. Some final chips would fall if he did not stop Charlie Henderson. And they could be the most terribly relevant ones of his life.

———

His assistant, Kermit Cushing, began the day in the office by going over the day's schedule and priorities, the way assistants had started most every day in every office since Bruce Conn Clark had become important enough to have an office and an assistant. The assistants had all been young men with names like Kermit Cushing since the White House job and Sharon had insisted on a ban against young female assistants. Bruce found it actually more convenient for traveling and for lessening rumors, distractions and temptations, so he had continued the male-only policy on his own ever since.

"Lunch with Count Lambsdorff at the German ambassador's residence," said Kermit Cushing to Bruce. They were sitting on the same couches Bruce and Jay Buckner had done their business on the night before. Cushing, a dark-haired Yale summa cum laude of twenty-five in a dark gray suit, was speaking from an open blue cardboard folder. "Two meetings this morning before lunch—one at ten with Mr. Khalidi of Egypt on the General Motors matter, the second at eleven with the Pakistani ambassador. He still wants a meeting with JCPenney."

"JCPenney is not interested in opening stores in Islamic countries with strongly anti-American mobs," said Bruce. "I have told them before and, for my usual fee, I will tell them again."

Kermit Cushing continued. "Dinner at the Westin, black tie, for the Senate majority leader. You will be the third to toast, and a suggested draft is in the folder. Two walk-through receptions beforehand, both downtown. Do you want to change here or at the apartment?"

"The apartment."

"There will be time."

Bruce nodded. Under the established procedure the blue folder would be handed to him when the brief briefing was over. In it were the details of each of the day's events—guest lists, agendas, texts, talking points, references back to previous meetings and statements that had been prepared by the various specialists in the firm of Clark & Associates.

"We have a request for a book blurb," said Cushing. "It is about the rise of democracy in Southeast Asia and is by a man named Richard Dreyer. It came as usual with the bound galleys."

"Dick Dreyer worked for me at State," said Bruce. "But I have neither the time nor interest in reading his book. So do me a nonread blurb, something like 'No one knows more about the rise of democracy in Southeast Asia than Richard Dreyer.' I want to be able to pass a flutter on whether I read the book."

He got only a blank stare of obedience from Cushing. Flutter. He had just said "flutter." This kid, thought Bruce, hasn't a clue as to what he was talking about. Flutter. My God, he thought, I haven't used or even thought of that word in years. It just popped out.

"Yes, sir," said Cushing and moved on to the next item. "We've had an initial inquiry from *Face the Nation* for this Sunday. They want you to debate taking military action against Iraq."

"Debate with whom?"

"Kissinger, Brzezinski, Schlesinger, someone like that."

"Only with Kissinger and Schlesinger. Brzezinski was never of cabinet rank."

"There are several new social invitations in the folder. Nothing that requires special attention. Marcus of Ward and Cronin has three speaking-engagement proposals for late spring. All meet the financial and transportation requirements and can be accommodated in your schedule. One is in Brighton and could be added to your London and Brussels itinerary. The dates work." Ward and Cronin was Bruce's lecture agent.

No response was necessary or expected from Bruce. Cushing

closed the blue folder. "The phone-call list is, of course, ready and waiting."

"Of course," said Bruce. "Speaking of calls, if a Mr. Jayson calls, please put him right through. It is about a personal matter."

"Something I could handle for you, sir?" said Cushing.

"Not unless you wish to have sex with a British duchess," said Bruce ever so casually. "Mr. Jayson is the cover name of an old friend with many contacts and interests in Europe."

Cushing's face colored. And he left the office.

Bruce went over behind his desk and sat down. He felt strangely happy and young. Here he was using words like *flutter* and *cover* and making up good clean lies like he still did it every day for a living.

But what happened at the Hyatt? Where are you, Jaybird? How did it go? Tell me something, Jaybird. No, no, Bruce scolded himself. His CIA trainer at Camp Perry had said over and over, impatience has killed more people than cancer, heart disease and car bombs put together.

He picked up the telephone and said to a woman in an outer office, "Good morning. Let's begin the calls."

In a matter of a few seconds, his phone buzzed and he was on the line with the president of Mexico about how to get presidential and congressional support for a North American free-trade zone.

———

He turned on the radio in the backseat. He fooled with the dial until he found a newscast. But it was only national and international news. The trip from his office to the residence of the German ambassador on Foxhall Road in Wesley Heights was a quick ten minutes, so he was there and out of the limo before he could find and thus hear any local news. Jaybird had not called. Bruce's own meetings and other calls had kept him from listening to the radio in the office.

The German ambassador was a delightful foreign-ministry professional who had come to Washington as the representative of West Germany and in a matter of a few months saw his diplomatic mission expand to include all of Germany. It had all happened so fast, so unpredictably, so beautifully, that everyone, including Bruce, enjoyed rejoicing and marveling with the Germans about it all. Bruce's firm also did some consulting work for BMW, and he had known Otto Count Lambsdorff, chairman of the Free Democratic Party in Germany, for many years.

There were twenty people at the luncheon. A good group, by Bruce's judgment, and he knew the full guest list before he came or he would not have come. It included Treasury Secretary Brady, Senator David Pryor of Arkansas, Bruce's friend Jim Schlesinger, as well as Al Haig, who Bruce found delightful but usually wrong, and Paul Nitze, delightful and usually right.

The food, like all German food, was heavy—too heavy for Bruce. But he nibbled at the dufferin first course and at the leg of lamb "Chatillon" with spring vegetables main course. He passed completely on the chocolate mousse and took not even one sip of the 1985 Avelsbacher Altenberg Riesling white wine, the 1985 Château Tour du Terre Bordeaux red or the Henkell Trocken champagne.

His days with the Agency were already very much on his mind, and passing up two good wines and a champagne heightened it. As a young CIA warrior living, as he and his colleagues liked to say, "close to the blade," he ate and drank well and often. He never heard of any CIA agent ever being criticized or even questioned about the cost of a meal, a drink or a hotel room. Fighting the secret wars for freedom could not be done on an expense-account mentality, said and practiced the Agency's chiefs.

The lunch was around a long dining-room table, nine people on each side and one at each end. The ambassador touched a fork to his glass shortly after everyone was seated and made a few introductory remarks to and about Count Lambsdorff. The count, as articulate in English as he was in German, responded with a few words about his old friends at the table, including most particularly Bruce, who was given the position of honor on the count's left. For fifty minutes, as everyone else ate, the count discussed the prospects for war in the Persian Gulf, the chances of Gorbachev staying on for long as president of the Soviet Union, the need to bring the French to their senses so a deal on agricultural subsidies could be made on the Uruguay Round trade talks and, of course, the glories and the difficulties of making Germany whole again.

It was the kind of Washington luncheon Bruce had been going to for years and about the only kind he really enjoyed anymore. It was the company of mostly equal-ranked and -minded people in a pleasant setting where things that mattered were discussed. And it was always over by two o'clock.

His limo had barely turned south out of the ambassador's driveway on Foxhall Road when he turned the radio on again. This time he heard a WTOP newsman's voice say what he so dearly had wanted to hear:

"D.C. police are investigating an explosion this morning at the Hyatt Regency Hotel on New Jersey Avenue Northwest. A small explosive device of undetermined origin detonated in a guest room on the hotel's eighth floor. No one was injured."

Good work, Jaybird.

Jaybird and Brucebear were an unlikely pairing, but unlikely pairings were what successful covert operations were all about. Two guys walking around together with the same accents, same mannerisms, same cut of clothes usually added up to two cops, two agents or two spooks, and a blown operation.

Jay Buckner, as a young man of thirty-two, wore his hair long in a ponytail and dressed in dirty blue jeans and a wrinkled shirt with missing buttons when he arrived in Lisbon. It would be assumed at a glance that he was a hippie, an antiwar American who had come to Portugal to avoid going to Vietnam. He rented a room over a small grocery store in an old part of the city called Lapa. It was an area sprinkled with small working-class bars and restaurants that was next door to an exclusive residential area that included the residences of several ambassadors, among them that of the ambassador from the United States of America.

Bruce, well dressed and short-haired, was in Lisbon with an IBM cover, working as a sales representative trying to bring the Portuguese into the very beginnings of the computer age. He actually went to the downtown office of IBM every morning and even made some calls on potential clients, particularly in the Portuguese government. But he also took trips out into the countryside looking for computer customers and did a lot of socializing during both the long Lisbon lunches and the late dinners. He particularly liked the small cafés in the Alfama, Lisbon's old town. His Agency assignment was to help run three spies, two in the Soviet embassy, a third in the Chinese. There were also occasional special assignments and some regular baby-sitting work on other "human assets" who came from Spain, France and Italy for R and R and debriefings at rented villas along the coast south of Lisbon. Bruce was fully covert, meaning he was never to have any contact with the economic attaché at the United States embassy, who was actually the CIA station chief in Lisbon. All of Bruce's orders came by other means, sometimes by couriers posing as American tourists or businessmen just passing through.

Jay Buckner was the first hippie courier Bruce had ever encountered and he was also the first from technical services, although the two of them had worked together several times before on pre-arranged projects. Jay's job this time was to help Bruce carry out the assignment he was giving him, which involved a little bit of friendly kidnapping and terrorism.

Bruce and Jay met at one of those Alfama cafés, seemingly by accident as two Americans with nothing more in common than their Americanism. The mission was to get a Bulgarian secret-police agent out to one of the rented villas long enough for a very senior Agency man from Washington to turn the Bulgarian and leave him in place. The Agency had something extremely incriminating to use as blackmail material on the guy, who was in Lisbon as an escort/watchdog for a group of four Bulgarian trade officials.

The agent had already been softened up by a CIA asset in Sofia and was told to expect something more in Lisbon.

The plan was simple enough. Jay was to cause the Bulgarians' car to have a mechanical problem on their sightseeing trip north of the city to the Atlantic beaches. Along would come Bruce in a rented car to stop and offer them help. Even if unable to speak Bulgarian and all other languages the guy spoke, Bruce would offer by sign language or whatever means to drive the agent to the next town for help. Jay would be waiting there in another car and he would whisk off the Bulgarian to a nearby house for his rendezvous with blackmail. The agent would then be returned to the downed car accompanied by a mechanic. Jay, of course, would be the mechanic and would fix the car. The whole thing would take less than an hour and the four other Bulgarians would never know what happened.

Everything went according to plan until they got back to the town and the three of them—Jay, Bruce and the Bulgarian—were walking back to Bruce's car. The Bulgarian, a man in his early thirties, had a sudden change of heart or something and pulled a pistol and started shooting. His second shot tore into Bruce's right shoulder. There was no third shot because Jay killed the Bulgarian by breaking his nose and then shoving the broken bone fragments up into his brain all in one quick one-two wham with his strong right hand. It was one of several standard hand-to-hand combat methods to kill somebody then taught in the CIA and the United States military.

Bruce, bleeding slightly but not in serious danger, then calmly drove back to Lisbon to a hospital on a back road while Jay threw the Bulgarian off a cliff into the Atlantic Ocean and proceeded back to the Lisbon airport and caught a plane for Madrid and then on to London. Neither ever found out what happened to the four Bulgarian trade officials waiting along the side of the road.

The hole in Bruce's shoulder was not large but it left a scar about the size of a quarter that was still there twenty-four years later. At the time CIA doctors thought the wound serious enough to keep him out of the field for a while, so Bruce quit the Agency and, as they say, the rest is history.

It was all there in his head as well as his shoulder as he went to the phone that evening in his Watergate apartment. He was in the dressing room putting on his tuxedo for the Westin dinner. It was three minutes after seven-thirty P.M., right on schedule. He let it ring twice. It stopped. Then, in twenty seconds, it started ringing again. This time he picked it up on the third ring.

"Clark here," he said.

"Jaybird here," said Jay Buckner.

They talked only a few minutes and only in generalities about what had happened at a Washington hotel that morning and what would happen tomorrow in Martinsburg, West Virginia. It would have been impossible for anyone who might have overheard the conversation to figure out what they were talking about.

———

Bruce believed there were only two men in Washington who were a success at being funny intentionally and both were named Mark. Mark Russell, a professional satirist who did humor for a living, and Mark Shields, a syndicated columnist and TV commentator who did it on the side. The fact that both Marks were involved in the Westin dinner was one of the reasons Bruce agreed to also offer a toast. It was in honor of Senator George Mitchell of Maine, the Democratic majority leader, but the proceeds went to the National Spina Bifida Association. Bruce was careful to spread his appearances and presence among and throughout both parties and all wings and factions. He had never wanted anybody ever to be able to honestly question anything he said on partisan grounds. Bruce Conn Clark was a man of ideas and action, by God. He said and did things because he thought they were right, not for any political purpose. It was an obsession he shared with Paul Nitze and Jim Schlesinger. Listen to me because I am smart and I care, was the message and the attitude Bruce had spent his years since the Agency cultivating. And it was one that he wished to go to the grave with.

Mark Shields, who was the emcee, opened the evening with some terrific digs at the Democratic party, the Republican party, the Senate, the state of Maine and the United States buildup in the Gulf. His biggest laugh came when he said the emir of Kuwait and the king of Saudi Arabia had just adopted the same new national anthem for their countries. And he sang a cappella the first two lines from it— "Onward Christian soldiers, marching on to war/With the cross of Jesus going on before." Mark Russell later brought down the house with a musical rendition of Vice President Quayle addressing a group of marines on their way to the Gulf about what to expect. To the tune of "Battle Hymn of the Republic," Russell sang about his eyes seeing the glory of the National Guard, carbon paper, paper clips, weekends in Indianapolis, bloomers in Bloomington, Daddy on the telephone. Mark Russell was a much better singer than Mark Shields.

There were five speakers, Bruce being the last before Mitchell's response. Bruce followed his rules for such appearances. Be brief, be light, don't talk about yourself and don't read it. He waited his turn there at the head table with confidence. He knew that the other four speakers would violate at least one of those rules and that as a result he would get the winks and the quiet assurances at the end that he was far and away the best. He knew it because that was what always happened.

He was also struck sitting there looking out into the hotel ballroom of six hundred or so people that he could not remember the last time he went to a banquet of any size at which he was not at the head table and/or a featured speaker or presence. It was another part of his life as Bruce Conn Clark that he enjoyed very much, another one that he was determined to go to his grave with intact.

And another he could not allow Charlie Henderson to destroy.

Sorry, Charlie, he said to himself. Sorry, Charlie. Wasn't there some kind of TV commercial several years ago with "Sorry, Charlie" in it? Bruce couldn't remember for sure. He had never had much time to watch television, except for the news, *MacNeil/ Lehrer* and the Sunday talk shows.

———————

Bruce got the word on what happened to Charlie and his Wag-oneer at Kearneysville late the next afternoon in the office conference room. He was finishing a one-on-one lunch with the Austrian ambassador to the United States when Kermit Cushing came in to see if he would take a call from "Mr. Jayson." Bruce nodded and without leaving the room picked up the phone on a table and said: "Clark here."

"Jaybird here," said Buckner.

"I assume all went well," Bruce said.

"You assume correctly."

"Anything of a collateral nature pending?"

"Nothing."

"Thank you. Maybe we could talk later?"

"At your beck," said Buckner.

Bruce hung up, knowing and pleased that Charlie Henderson had once again been scared but with nothing of a collateral nature pending, meaning Charlie had not been injured or killed.

He returned to the table, freshened the ambassador's red wine and resumed their conversation. The lunch had been catered by Le Pavillon, Bruce's favorite French restaurant in Washington. The government of Austria had hired Bruce to consult with them on how to find a way to get the president of Austria, Kurt Wald-heim, off the official undesired list of the United States of America. Before Charlie Henderson reentered his life Bruce was scheduled to do the consulting directly with Waldheim and the Austrian prime minister in Vienna for thirty thousand dollars plus first-class air fare and a five-star hotel suite for him and an assistant.

For fifteen thousand dollars he instead told the ambassador: "You have only two options, I am sorry to say. You can get yourself a new president or you can wait for all people to forget World War Two and the Nazis."

"There is nothing else to do?" said the ambassador, a tall, jolly, well-dressed man in his sixties.

"Nothing, sir. Absolutely nothing. No president, no secretary of state, no Congress could ever reverse the situation without some stunning new piece of information such as proof that Waldheim was actually born in a manger and after the end of World War Two."

In order to make the ambassador and his government feel they got their money's worth, Bruce devoted two hours to the lunch and shared his insights fully about the situation in the Gulf and the problems of Mikhail Gorbachev. It was the least he could do for fifteen thousand dollars.

Bruce called Charlie just before five o'clock. Charlie seemed surprised at the call. Good. And, like everyone who receives a Bruce Conn Clark invitation, he quickly agreed to meet for lunch tomorrow at the G Street Club.

Bruce talked to Jay immediately afterward and told him to move it onto the next phase. The phase in which Charlie would be guided into figuring out who it was that was trying to kill him.

He also told Cushing to inform *Face the Nation* that he would be available Sunday morning to debate Kissinger about the advisability of military action in the Gulf.

Bruce arrived twelve minutes early at the G Street Club. Jay had missed Charlie somewhere along the way and had called from a pay phone at the Duffields station for some instructions. Get in your car and drive to Washington and the G Street Club as fast as you can, were the instructions from Bruce. Then trail Charlie from there. Jay said the telephone surveillance at Hillmont had not picked up anything to the contrary, so Bruce was certain Charlie would keep the appointment and assumed Charlie had come to Washington on an earlier train or by some other means.

Bruce was not certain about what Charlie might do from here on out. And that, to Bruce's own amazement, excited him as much as it concerned him. Maybe more.

Bruce was met at the club door by a black man in a tuxedo and white gloves who knew that the white man who had arrived was Bruce Conn Clark. The man's name was Johnson and it was only by that last name that he was ever called by Bruce or anyone else. Johnson did not ask Bruce what he wanted to drink because he already knew. He did not ask him where he wanted to wait because he already knew. It would be in one of the small alcove writing rooms that contained only two overstuffed antique chairs, a writing table and a few old leather-bound books on an end table. Johnson showed Bruce to the room and then fetched him a plain club soda over ice with a twist of lemon. Bruce, because he went early to everything, came prepared for the wait. He had a small brown leather attaché case with him and out of it he pulled a rough draft of an op-ed page piece he had written for *The Washington Post* on what a post–Gulf War Middle East might look like. Bruce had written it himself and now he would edit it himself. The ability to write coherently, concisely and quickly, he believed, was the single most important skill there was. It applied to everyone. Doctors and lawyers who could write had an edge over their peers, as did preachers, spies, diplomats, salesmen and all the rest.

At five minutes after noon Johnson told Bruce he had a telephone call. Bruce picked up the phone on the writing table.

Bruce listened to Charlie Henderson's explanation. Phony, obviously. Why wait until now to call? Where was he calling from? What is Charlie up to? The old warrior is warrioring, that's what.

For the first time in years Bruce Conn Clark felt as young as he looked. And he guessed Charlie probably did, too.

Where are you, Charlie Henderson? I'm as good as you are, Charlie Henderson.

At the limo in front of the club, Jay Buckner, dressed in a gray suit, came up to Bruce. "Follow me," was all Bruce said to him.

Bruce got in the backseat of his limo and told his driver to head north on Twenty-first Street. Jay went across the street to his car.

Follow me where? thought Bruce after they had gone a block. To a restaurant. Sure. They could talk in private there. Bruce recalled that Jay Buckner was a man who saw missed meals as a missed opportunity to enjoy himself. And he doubted from the looks of him that much had changed. They had not kept up a going relationship after Bruce left the Agency. How can an up-and-coming international whiz stay in touch with a career CIA technical-services man while making the trip of life from think-tank senior fellow to White House aide, foreign affairs magazine editor, undersecretary of state, national security adviser and, finally, secretary of state? Even if they had been more of like minds and backgrounds it would have been difficult.

What restaurant? He thought he remembered that Buckner was a fiend for Tex-Mex food. But Bruce hated it.

"Turn left at Mass Avenue and head toward Wisconsin," he told his driver.

Then he took down the car phone from its holder and dialed Kermit Cushing at the office.

"My luncheon engagement fell through," Bruce said. "I should be back at the office by two o'clock."

There was a long period in his life when he would have had to tell his assistant or a White House or State Department operator where he would be and for how long and why. No more. Kermit Cushing did not ask where Mr. Clark would be for the next hour and a half or so because it was not his job to ask—or to know.

What restaurant? He thought about Germaine's on Wisconsin. There was also Primavera, an Italian restaurant right at the corner of Mass and Wisconsin. Bruce had not been there in a while but he remembered it fondly for its terrific garlic bread and gnocchi. But that would be too much for lunch.

He glanced out the back window. Jay Buckner was not in the car right behind but, of course, he would not be. He would be a couple of cars back, maybe more. Standard procedure.

The limo passed by the Islamic temple and over the Rock Creek Bridge heading up the hill past the Brazilian embassy on the left, the former Iranian embassy, which was taken over and still owned by the United States government, on the right. Then came the South Africans next door, the British complex and the Naval Observatory with the vice-president's house on the left. It brought back Mark Russell's stinging ridicule of Quayle at the Westin dinner and Bruce's own private belief that it was an appalling outrage that a man of Dan Quayle's limited experience and ability was the vice-president of the United States of America. The possibility of war in the Persian Gulf just heightened Bruce's anxieties about it and his anger at George Bush for being so insecure that he had to select such an insignificant lightweight as his running-mate. Bruce believed—again, most privately—that history would be harsher on Bush for choosing Quayle than for any other thing he did. War or no war, depression or no depression, pestilence or no pestilence, what else or no what else.

It was then that Bruce knew exactly where he was going. There would be no lunch. He wasn't hungry and Jay Buckner could afford to miss a meal.

He told his driver to turn right when he got to Wisconsin Avenue, go north one block to Woodley, turn right along the north side of the Washington Cathedral and then left onto Thirty-sixth Street and start looking for a parking space. The driver found one around the corner on Macomb Street two blocks up. This was Cleveland Park. Bruce had never owned or lived in a real house in Washington—not even in Georgetown—because without children and most of the time without wives there was no need. But if he had ever had a house it would have been in Cleveland Park, a district of big old houses built mostly in the early 1900s by friends and associates of Grover Cleveland. It had since been inhabited mostly by liberal Democrats and overpaid pundits.

"When the man in the gray suit comes," said Bruce to his driver, "tell him I have gone to see the Good Shepherd. He will understand."

The driver touched his right hand to the bill of his cap as if to salute and Bruce strode with gusto toward the Washington Cathedral.

"How long has it been since I have been in here?" said Jay Buckner. He took the small pew to the left. Bruce was already in the larger one in the front row. Both spoke in quiet flat tones that did not carry.

"I was just thinking the same thing about myself," said Bruce. "Good God, I think it's been twenty-one years at least."

"Careful the way you throw around the word *God*, please."

"I did a sorry little Czech coding clerk right in this very pew," Bruce said. "She wanted us to bring out her mother."

"You screwed her?"

"No! I interviewed her. I never screwed the assets, Mr. Buckner. Never."

"Bullshit, Mr. Clark. I never met a covert type who could keep his pants on."

"I never knew a tech-services man who knew how to put his pants on."

They both laughed. We're like two little boys, thought Bruce. What am I doing here? I am one of America's most distinguished diplomats and upper-crusts. Why am I giggling in the Chapel of the Good Shepherd at the Washington Cathedral with a West Virginia real estate salesman?

"I even wired this place once," Buckner said. "The mike was right over there under your pew on the left side."

"You could go to hell for bugging God's house, sir."

"It was in the interests of national security. A Brit agent from down the street was meeting a Norwegian KGB plant but we didn't trust the Brit. Something like that."

It was always Something Like That, thought Bruce. And it was always fun. The scarier and tougher and crazier, the better. Horace Greeley said, "Go West, young man." Bruce would say, "Be a spy, young man."

"I appreciate your doing all of this for me," Bruce said. "I really do."

"It was good Sonny wanted to go to Harvard."

It sure was. Bruce had not heard from or thought about Jay Buckner until one morning eighteen months ago when a letter from Buckner turned up in a morning blue folder. Jay's youngest son, who was about to graduate from Penn State, was interested in going on to graduate school at the John F. Kennedy School of Government at Harvard. Bruce was on the JFK board and would he mind writing some kind of I-don't-know-the-kid-but-he-comes-from-good-stock kind of recommendation letter? Bruce got four or five such requests a month and he usually complied, as he did for Jay Buckner, alias Jaybird.

Then, after being stunned at DeCarlo's by Charlie Henderson, Bruce realized he needed some help. He remembered the letter from Jay and recalled vaguely from the letterhead that he lived somewhere in West Virginia. He had the letter retrieved and called Jay. Someone not of the Agency would probably not understand how and why Jay Buckner would receive a request for his special kind of help so favorably so quickly. The fact that it came from Bruce Conn Clark also helped, which Bruce realized when he called. *No* was a word he seldom heard.

"Can't say no to the one and only Bruce Conn Clark," said Jay now in the Chapel of the Good Shepherd.

"We haven't talked about any kind of payment. Let's do it now."

"On the house, Brucebear."

"No, no. Lawyers and whores don't give it away, neither should you."

"I saved your ass once, I'll save it again. What happened to Charlie?"

Bruce told him about the call at 12:05.

"I'm sure he didn't say where he was, right?" Jay asked.

"He said he was in Winchester. But I doubt it."

"Maybe we should have gone all of the way when we had the chance."

"Wrong."

"Is he likely to come after the Brucebear now?" Jay asked. "You want some protection?"

Bruce did not answer immediately. He tried to imagine what he would do if he was in Charlie Henderson's shoes. Okay, Bruce Conn Clark is trying to have me killed. Do I go after Clark or do I try to find out why he's trying to have me killed? He said to Jay: "I can't see Charlie doing that. Not yet at least. Covert types don't go around killing people anyhow. No offense, Jaybird."

"Now what?"

"Find him."

"Then what?"

"Watch him."

"Aye, aye. Lunch?"

"Pass."

They stood. Bruce remained in place as Jay moved past him up the narrow aisle toward the exit.

"Here," said Bruce, holding out two twenty-dollar bills toward Bruce.

"Now, that is an offense, Brucebear," said Jay Buckner, his voice still quiet. "I can buy my own food."

"Sorry," said Bruce, realizing too late what a stupid thing he had just done.

"If you want to do me a real service, get the Agency to build their new facility in Jefferson County, West Virginia. It'll make me rich."

"I'll see what I can do. I know the chairmen of the two committees."

He meant it when he said it, but five minutes after Buckner was gone he realized that would not be a smart thing to do. Even a casual word to the chairman of the Senate or House intelligence committees that might tie him to Jay Buckner would not be a smart thing to do. There was no telling how this was all going to work itself out.

Another one of the pleasures of being Bruce Conn Clark was having good clothes. The closet in his Watergate apartment bedroom would make envious any male person who could wear 17-35 shirts, 44-long suits and sport coats, 35-waist trousers and 10B shoes. One of his biggest secrets had to do with his shirts. Fifteen years ago, just before the Sadat-Begin and Camp David breakthroughs, Bruce went to Egypt on a special diplomatic mission. He spent two delightful days and evenings with President Anwar Sadat, one of the nattiest dressers in his and all other parts of the world. Bruce, making small talk over a lunch, singled out for particular praise the president's dress shirts. Sadat said he had a man in London who made them and asked Bruce what size he wore. Bruce told him and three months later a shipment of eighty dress shirts was delivered to Bruce's apartment in Washington.

They were a mix of sixteen different colors and shades and five different collar styles. Half were French cuffs. Bruce decided after two vodkas on the rocks and two hours of intense solitary worry to keep them and tell no one. United States government regulations forbid the acceptance of any gift worth more than fifty dollars. Bruce concluded that each of the eighty shirts was worth about forty-eight dollars and he would look upon each as a single gift. To have returned the shirts would have insulted Sadat; to have turned them in to the United States government for destruction or to rot in a government warehouse would have been an insult to his sanity.

It was a source of pride with Bruce that he could still wear the Sadat shirts, even though he had only a dozen or so left. He put on one now, a French cuff model that was pale yellow with a white collar. He was going to dinner in Georgetown at the home of Danielle and Bill Hollowell, the syndicated columnist. The phoned invitation to the office said there would be twelve people including Bruce, all of them acceptable to Bruce except one. The exception was a magazine editor named Jonathan Perry. Bruce agreed to come on the promise that Perry would be seated far away from him. He always demanded to know the guest list because he had had his fill of showing up at small, intimate dinner parties to discover he was going to spend the evening with an old enemy or somebody who wanted to be a new friend by showing his or her brilliance with a plan for making peace with the Khmer Rouge or some such.

He enjoyed going to the Hollowells. Danielle was a gorgeous blonde who took care of herself and of Bruce at dinner parties by always putting him between the best and the brightest women present. Bill was a bit of a self-important blowhard for Bruce's taste, but he never used anything he heard over his own dinner table and he told terrific stories. When he was secretary of state, Bruce loved showing up at their house in the wake of the sirens and flashing lights of a motorcade. Having people with guns and earpieces parting the traffic and the world for you was an experience that Bruce truly relished and enjoyed. And missed. It made him understand forever why there are so many people in American politics who keep running for president time after time after time. It's because of Motorcade Syndrome, as Shields or somebody called it. It was a contagious disease and it was terminal.

The dinner, like 90 percent of all catered Washington dinner parties, was lamb and a fish course with all the trimmings. It came with a free-for-all conversation about whether the United States should take military action to get Iraq out of Kuwait. Hollowell entertained with some insider stuff he had heard about how scary Bush was with his need to prove he was tough and courageous enough to order America into war. A Democratic senator who wanted more time for sanctions to work argued the Eisenhower point that sometimes patience requires the most courage of all. The deputy secretary of state, who was sitting directly across from Bruce, vehemently disagreed. So did the Czechoslovakian ambassador to the United States, who argued that if the United States does not use its superpowers to contain land-thirsty tyrants, no small nation in the world will ever be safe. It was only when Bruce talked, agreeing quietly but forcefully with the pro-sanctions position of the senator, that everyone at the table fell silent. Everyone except Jonathan Perry. He was a lightweight sociology professor of no special talent or accomplishment who owned and edited the magazine *The New World* because his wife was a shoe-company heiress who bought it for him. He was a joke in all circles except those that believed money was important. Perry was an occasional dinner guest at the Hollowells' soley because his magazine published a long think piece by Bill Hollowell once a month.

"You epitomize the softies who have run our foreign policy the last twenty years," said Perry to Bruce from across and down the table.

"Did you ever get an invitation?" Bruce said to Perry. "That is the real question Washington wants answered."

He then turned to the wife of the senator on his left to make damned sure Perry and everyone else knew that the answer to that question was of absolutely no interest to him or anyone else.

Perry, what Bruce would call a predictable fool's fool, had made himself even more foolish by writing a recent column accusing the producers of talk shows, particularly on public television and radio, of blacklisting him for his strong pro-Israel views. It was embarrassing incoherence that only the owner of a publication could have brought to public print.

Danielle Hollowell hit a glass with a spoon and said, "Shall we go to the library for coffee?"

Leaving parties whenever he wished was another of the perks for Bruce in being who and what he was. He exercised it at 10:45 and was back in his apartment by 11:00 to take the prearranged call from Jay Buckner.

"The tap is working. He called home and said he was in Philadelphia," Buckner said.

"Do you believe it?"

"Nope."

"Where, then?"

"He could be anywhere from home in bed to the Howard Johnson's across from you at the Watergate."

Bruce smiled. "You mean the one our friend Hunt and company used to bug the Democrats?"

"Same. It could also be used as a sniper's nest to get you, Brucebear."

"We'll talk again tomorrow," Bruce said as he hung up. He was still smiling.

This could get very interesting before it's over, he thought.

What are you doing, Charlie Henderson?

"Lancaster, Pennsylvania, this time. But no motel in the area has him checked in," said Jay Buckner. "He could be in China."

"Thanks," said Bruce.

"Now what?"

"Keep listening."

They made arrangements to talk again.

"Fuck you, Mikhail Gorbachev!" Bruce shouted into the empty Watergate elevator on his way downstairs a few minutes later. It was a very un-Bruce thing to do. Nobody would have believed Bruce Conn Clark went around shouting things like that in elevators.

It was Sunday morning and Bruce was on his way to the studios of CBS to appear on *Face the Nation* with Lesley Stahl. There was a time when he played the three Sunday talk shows off against each other like a three-way cockfight. He came when he wanted to come and always under conditions that suited him and only him. There were never any negotiations about other guests or even about other times. These days he still had some power to wheel and deal, but it was limited. That was why he had only one invitation for this Sunday and he had to share the time with Henry Kissinger, somebody Bruce thoroughly liked and mostly disagreed with. Bruce thought Kissinger was one of the best minds he had ever encountered and was in an intellectual class on foreign and security issues with a small select group that included Nitze, Schlesinger and Brzezinski. He found it appalling that the Bush administration chose to ignore such great talent that was right there under its nose. And that included himself, of course. He was still waiting for a call from Bush or Baker to invite him to have a quiet conversation about Iraq. Schlesinger, Brzezinski, Nitze and Kissinger were, too, he was sure.

But, of course, if Charlie Henderson had his way, there would never ever be even a possibility of his being used as an elder statesman by any president or even as a guest on a Sunday talk show.

That was what was on his mind during the drive to M Street and CBS, not how he would try to "take" Henry on sanctions versus military action in the Gulf.

He wondered how close Charlie was getting, how long it would be before he heard from him. He felt helpless to do anything to stop it, and for the first time he started considering the possibility that Jay Buckner was right. Somebody might have to die before this was over.

You or me, Charlie?

Then he remembered the name of Clay Reynolds, Angleton's man who investigated and fluttered him. Hadn't Reynolds, like Jay about his son, written once about something? He would get Cushing to scrub the files on it in the morning. Scrub the files. There, it had happened again. Another of those Agency terms popped back.

He had Cushing use a "memoirs" story in extending the invitation for lunch. It happened at the Cosmos Club, a famous old mansionlike private club on Massachusetts Avenue west of Dupont Circle that Bruce had always refused to join until they had finally voted to admit women members last year. Before that, women could come to lunch only as guests, and then they had had to enter through the side door. Bruce believed that men who felt that way about women were political and moral idiots, the kind he had no wish to eat meals with.

"I am trying to refresh my memory on some details of my life," he said to Clay Reynolds, the man across the lunch table from him. "Years can stunt the memory."

"Especially in your case, since so much has happened in your years," said Reynolds. Bruce was used to people being tickled to death and nervous about being with him and Reynolds was no exception. He seemed to be perspiring more than the temperature in the room warranted and he ran some of his words together.

Bruce would never have recognized Reynolds. He had remembered him as a tall, thin man with a full head of dark black hair. Now he was a tall, heavy man with a bald head and a dark gray beard. The sweat was clearly visible on the head. Recognition in the club's lounge was no problem, of course, because Reynolds certainly knew Bruce Conn Clark when he saw him.

Bruce decided a little warming small talk was in order. So he got Reynolds's since-I-saw-you story, which was told quickly and dully. Reynolds said he had left the Agency in 1978 and gone with a security consulting firm that specialized in helping corporations protect their overseas employees and facilities from terrorists. A multinational insurance company that was a client took a liking to him and brought him in at a high-level position and now he was the CEO.

"I don't have to ask about what you've been up to," Reynolds said one breath after finishing his own report.

Reynolds was well into his chicken pot pie and on his second glass of white wine by the time Bruce brought it around to business. Two glasses of wine at lunch? Most unusual for Washington, thought Bruce. He, as was his habit, ordered a glass of wine to make his lunch companion feel comfortable but did not touch it. He had only a large shrimp salad to eat.

"I have always been curious about how you and Jim Angleton came to investigate me," said Bruce. "Now it's all a matter of such ancient history, so I assume there would be no problem in my knowing. Am I right?"

There was a problem. Bruce could tell from a glance at the top of Reynolds's head. But Reynolds's words said just the opposite. "You're right," he said.

"My brother is now a man in his eighties, retired, living the life of a stuffy old intellectual, so maybe you could put us both into the picture," said Bruce. "I might also want to put it in my memoirs."

Reynolds, peering first at the less than an inch of wine left in his glass, said: "I would have sworn you had already written those. In fact, I read them."

Bruce was ready for that one. His memoirs, *My Watch,* had, in fact, been published in 1985 and had even made it to number seven during a four-week run on *The New York Times* best-seller list.

"But that book, as you recall," he told Reynolds, "was mostly about my work as a diplomat. Now I would like to go beyond that into some other facets of my life."

Reynolds said: "Well, I am afraid I cannot help you on the CI investigation. I handled so many of those through the years, they are all a blur to me now."

"I can certainly understand that," Bruce said. "Do you happen to remember if the matter concerning me was something that was widely known outside CI?"

"I doubt it. We were airtight."

"Airtight, right."

"I do not recall that any of it came out during your confirmation hearings as secretary of state," Reynolds said. "Do I remember correctly?"

"You do. Good point."

"It would seem to me that if something was going to get out that was when it would have."

"Yes. But there was nothing serious involved in the investigation to get out, was there?"

"I guess not."

"Just a guess, Mr. Reynolds? After all, you were in charge. You were the one who was in charge of the investigation, the one who interviewed me."

"To repeat, sir, all of these things blur together. It has been a long time. You are important now, but at the time you were just one more covert man on which a routine CI check was made. Please remember, Mr. Angleton believed in checking everybody and everything."

"Yes, indeed."

Dessert arrived. Again, to make Reynolds comfortable Bruce had ordered a piece of German chocolate cake, the day's special. Reynolds had it with a glob of French vanilla ice cream on it. Bruce suddenly wondered if this man was eating and drinking like this out of nervousness or habit. He was in his late sixties like Bruce. Did he not know this kind of stuff was bad for the heart and everything else? It is strange what irrelevant things a person will think about at times like this. He was also struck by the fact that so many important matters in life are resolved over meals. He and his second wife decided to go their separate ways at a three-hundred-dollar dinner at Le Pavillon. He was offered the secretary of state's job while trying to eat a barbecued rib without getting the sauce on his light gray suit. He got the Israelis to agree to stop the bombardment of Beirut while munching on a piece of toast in Tel Aviv.

Bruce used his fork to play with his piece of German chocolate cake. What would be the harm in taking a bite? One bite certainly is not going to hurt me, for God's sake.

He took the bite, chewed it slowly, swallowed and said, "Terrific cake." What followed was a silly and silent search of his memory for the last time he had actually had a piece of German chocolate cake in his mouth. Was it in 1982 at a diner on the West Side of Manhattan? Right. He had gone there with a famous woman writer he was dating at the time.

"Terrific cake," said Reynolds, his mouth full of it.

Bruce was preparing to ask the question he really came to ask. His many years on the line in the Agency, but mostly since as a diplomat from the lowest to the highest level, had helped him develop his own sense of the "flutter." He pretty much believed it was possible for him to look across the table—a conference table as well as one on which food was being served—and tell whether the person talking to him was telling the truth. He had through his career made several major decisions on that basis. Once he asked a mid-level military leader of Panama if any officials of his government were involved in drug trafficking. No, the military man replied indignantly, and Bruce knew it was a lie and told the people at State, Defense and the DEA back in Washington just that. The guy's name was Manuel Noriega.

"Just out of curiosity," said Bruce as he readied a second bite of cake for his mouth, "has anyone else contacted you lately about me and my time in the Agency?"

Reynolds was fully committed to his cake and ice cream, so most of what Bruce could see was the top of his head. Bruce watched it jerk from left to right and then back to the left in what was meant to be a negative shaking. "No," said Reynolds through the cake and ice cream.

It was clear he was lying. Seldom had a lie come through so loud and clear to Bruce's flutter. Reynolds's lie-telling skills were rusty. Also, CI people asked questions. They never had to answer anybody else's.

"I had heard that somebody was around asking about me," said Bruce ever so casually. "Something about a book an ex-Agency man wants to write about spooks who went on to do other things in their lives."

"Haven't heard a word about it," said Reynolds, still, according to Bruce's read, lying through his cake and ice cream.

"The guy's name is Henderson. Charlie Henderson. Does that name ring any bells?"

"No bells," said Reynolds.

Bruce's thoughts went immediately to how he should go to South Carolina. By charter or commercial?

———————

He placed the call at the prescribed time. It was from a Lear jet at fifteen thousand feet.

Jay reported: "He said he was going to Harrisburg but that's bullshit. He obviously knows we're listening. I've been watching the house. No sign of him. Nobody around Charles Town has seen him or heard from him. He's gone. If I were you I would be watching my back, Brucebear."

"Thanks."

"What's that I hear behind you?"

"I'm on a plane."

"Where to?"

"To work it all out with Charlie."

"You know where he is?"

"I think I do."

"Is he a threat to you? Do you need me?"

"No, thanks. I'll take it from here, Jaybird. I haven't had a chance yet to look into that West Virginia CIA property matter."

"No problem. Be careful. Henderson was good."

"So was I."

PART THREE

Charlie and Bruce

November 22–23, 1963

I t was sheer chance that Bruce Conn Clark and Charles Avenue
Henderson were both in Washington on November 22, 1963.
Charlie was there recuperating from his Berlin wound and arguing
about his next assignment. He was fighting an effort to move him
permanently to Langley as an intelligence analyst. Bruce had come
for a briefing on a special assignment in Pakistan involving some
Soviet military officers due over from Afghanistan. One of the
officers had signaled a Pakistani intelligence officer that he might
be interested in talking to the Americans.

Both worked in the Soviet Russia Division, the outfit within the
CIA that dealt with all covert activity toward the Soviets and the
Warsaw Pact. But Charlie and Bruce did not know each other
because they had never worked together. SRD, like most of the
Agency divisions then, was heavily compartmentalized. Everything was on a need-to-know basis, particularly when it came to
the names and even the appearances of fellow agents. The theory
was simply that the less you know the less you can tell if captured
and tortured. Jim Angleton and others in CI argued that it also

meant less for a mole or a potential traitor to know and thus to spill. The rule was strictly enforced with and among covert types like Charlie and Bruce because they were considered the most vulnerable both to capture and to temptation, operating out in the field under the most dangerous and difficult circumstances of any Agency officers.

Charlie spent the morning of November 22 at Bethesda Naval Hospital being examined one more time by a team of doctors who thought he was a naval officer who had been shot accidentally while cleaning a pistol aboard a ship in the Sea of Japan. The bullet had gone right through his stomach at a downward angle, entering just above the navel and out the back just above the buttocks. It narrowly missed his spine and other valuable and vital parts. The only lingering problem was with his small intestine, which had been nicked by the bullet on its way through. It was another X ray of them, complete with the awful barium cocktail, that was done on him this morning. "Looks good," was all some guy in a white coat told him when it was over. He knew it would be a couple of days before their report would find its circuitous way back to the CIA doctors at Langley.

They were through with him at 12:45, so he decided to get lunch somewhere in Bethesda before heading back across the river to Virginia and headquarters.

Bruce, getting ready for his Pakistan assignment, was in meetings all morning at Langley. First, two Afghanistan specialists used photographs, maps and other visual aids to help him understand the arcane politics of this Soviet satellite country that in some areas was as remote and backward as the fourteenth century. Then came the familiar team of Soviet army experts to update Bruce on who was currently where and why within the Soviet army. They broke for lunch at 12:15 and Bruce broke for the Georgetown Inn on Wisconsin Avenue two blocks north of M Street. He had a nooner appointment with one of the Soviet army briefers, a young woman with a Ph.D. from the University of Chicago. Bruce liked smart women, something his brother Duane often called his "phallic flaw."

<hr>

Charlie went from the naval hospital to the Hot Shoppe at the corner of Old Georgetown Road and Wisconsin Avenue, the major crossroads of Bethesda. Because he was by himself and because it was their busy lunchtime, the hostess asked if he minded sitting on a stool at the counter. No problem, he said, and he was sitting and ordering a few minutes later. He got a cheeseburger with everything and a Coke, primarily because those were the kinds of things that were hard to get elsewhere in the world. He ate and drank slowly. There was no reason to hurry back to Langley. All he would do is sit in a closed cubicle on the fourth floor reading intelligence summaries and suppositions about various KGB stations around the world.

At 1:35 Charlie took a ten-dollar bill out of his billfold and got ready to pay.

"Oh, my God! No!" It was a woman screaming. He looked back behind the counter. A waitress came running out of the kitchen. "Kennedy! They shot Kennedy!"

Another waitress started to cry. Charlie put the money on the counter and ran as fast as he could for his car. He turned on the motor and the radio and sped south on Wisconsin toward Langley.

<hr>

Bruce and the young woman Soviet army expert were in bed at the Georgetown Inn, under the covers but pretty much through with what they had come to do on this particular lunch break.

"How about something from room service, Dana dear?" Bruce

asked the Soviet army expert, who knew Bruce only as "Mark," his inside code name. Her real name was Dana Radnitz, and because she was an analyst who never left Langley, it was the one she used with everyone.

"I'd love it," she said. "A chef's salad and ice tea, maybe?"

"Why not," said Bruce. He picked up the telephone next to him and dialed room service. He listened impatiently for several rings. Finally a man answered, saying only, "Yes?"

"Room service?" Bruce asked.

"But the president has been shot! They shot the president in Dallas! Those bastards shot the president!"

Bastards? What bastards?

Within minutes both Bruce and Dana were in their respective clothes and cars racing across Key Bridge to the George Washington Parkway toward CIA headquarters.

———

The death of the president removed all walls from all compartments in the Soviet Russia Division. Bruce sprinted into the fourth-floor SRD office area with no concern about who saw him. Charlie did the same thing seven or eight minutes later.

It was in the office of Division Chief Tim Hancock that they met for the first time. There was a television set in there. Hancock and several others were gathered around it. Bruce, then Charlie, joined them. They nodded to each other and to the others but there was no shaking of hands, no exchanging of names. There was simply a quiet assumption that each and every person there was a trusted and honored member of the same fraternity or he wouldn't be there.

They watched while Walter Cronkite, Frank McGee, Chet Huntley and David Brinkley reported on the tragedy in Dallas.

"Right-wingers for sure?" Bruce said finally to the man standing next to him.

"That's the assumption. Nothing definite. They got Connally, too."

"Dead?" Bruce asked.

"Maybe not. Also a Secret Service man and a cop were hit."

Charlie had gotten a similar update when he arrived from Bethesda, although both had been following it on their car radios.

After a few minutes Hancock, an old-schooler from the OSS, took a phone call at his desk. Charlie watched him listen and then say only, "We're on it."

Hancock motioned for someone to turn down the sound on the television.

"We are looking for plots, gentlemen. What kind of right-wing possibilities might we have?"

"All ours are the other brand of wing," said someone Charlie did not recognize. He was an older man, about forty-five. Bruce knew him. He was Jimmy Jackson, Bruce's main contact man.

"Right," said Hancock. "Anyone?" He looked around the room to the approximately twelve men who were in it. Nobody had anything to add. If it was a right-wing plot, then the Soviet Russia Division would have nothing to contribute.

"Stay loose and ready," Hancock said to the room. "There is no telling where this thing could lead."

"Any arrests yet?"

Hancock motioned toward the television. "I think they're going to know as soon as we are. I assume the answer is no or they would know. Stay loose and ready, gentlemen."

It was more than an order to stay loose and ready. It was also one to get out of his office. In a silence that resembled that of mourners leaving a funeral chapel, they all filed out.

Bruce left with Jimmy Jackson and went back to Jackson's office to watch television with him. Charlie headed for his cubicle but then kept going to the office of J. Walton Morehead, his main contact man. There was a television in there and Walt would not mind his watching with him.

The television anchormen and their correspondents continued to report the news.

A rifle was found near a window of a building overlooking the assassination site. The building was called the Texas School Book Depository. The site was called Dealey Plaza, named after the founder of *The Dallas Morning News.* That was an irony. The current publisher of the *News,* a very right-wing paper, was Ted Dealey, the grandson of the founder. He hated John F. Kennedy. Dealey had recently written a nasty story about a White House meeting with a group of newspaper publishers in which he said the president acted like he was "riding Caroline's tricycle." The *News* had a run a full-page advertisement that very morning of November 22, said the TV reporters, accusing Kennedy of throwing away the country. There was a black border around the advertisement.

"Somebody ought to get that sonofabitch," Bruce said to Jimmy Jackson and two other men in Jackson's office. Bruce meant Dealey. The others showed agreement with their nods, although it was not clear if they understood what Bruce was saying.

Morehead made a similar comment in his office to Charlie and five other men with him.

"Somebody ought to dynamite the whole place," one of the others said.

"Amen," said Charlie, assuming he meant Dallas.

The news continued.

Mrs. Kennedy was unhurt. So were Vice President Johnson and his wife and Mrs. Connally. The earlier reports about a Secret Service agent and a cop being hit were not true. The Connallys had been in the car with the Kennedys. The Johnsons had been in another right behind them in the motorcade. All remained at Parkland Hospital in Dallas. Johnson would presumably be sworn in soon as president. Secretary of State Dean Rusk and Press Secretary Pierre Salinger had been on a flight to Japan to advance President Kennedy's trip to Japan in December when the assassination occurred. Their plane had turned around over the Pacific and was now on its way back to Washington. No one knew if the

Kennedy children had been told. The president's brothers, Attorney General Robert Kennedy and Senator Ted Kennedy, knew their brother was dead. Senator Kennedy had in fact been presiding over the Senate when the news came.

Then came the report of an arrest.

"A man who worked at the Texas School Book Depository," said Frank McGee on NBC. "He has been identified as Oswald. Lee Oswald."

Charlie heard a male shriek. "No! No! No!" somebody yelled.

Bruce, at the other end of the corridor, heard the same screams. Everybody in SRD heard them.

In a few seconds, the phones on Morehead's and Jimmy Jackson's desks rang. Each picked them up and said, "Yes, sir." Jimmy Jackson then said to Bruce and the men in his office, "Come with me. On the double." Morehead's face did all of his talking. It went from tan to a paper-tablet yellow. He merely motioned for Charlie and the others to follow him.

"Lee Harvey Oswald is the suspect's name," said Tim Hancock to the assembled group a very few seconds later. "He is a former marine who defected to the Soviet Union and came back. He may be one of ours."

No! No! No! screamed Charlie to himself.

So did Bruce to himself.

——————

The men and women of the Soviet Russia Division were divided up into teams. Charlie was put with a group assigned to focus on Oswald's time in the Soviet Union. Bruce's was told to explore everything Oswald did after he returned to the United States. There were others who looked at Oswald before and during his time in the Marine Corps, his family, all his foreign travel, his possible relationship with the Agency as well as the FBI, among other things. All computers were being programmed to glean out all that the Agency had on Oswald, Lee Harvey. Messages went out to every CIA station throughout the world to expedite all information they might have on Oswald and any known associates. Stations were told to "cover" all assets possible to probe for information about Oswald. CIA liaison personnel to the Defense and State departments were told to go to the Pentagon and the State Department and grab up everything they could on Oswald. They were also told to stay away from the FBI for now because they wouldn't get anything anyhow and it would only cause problems. The Central Intelligence Agency was second only to the Soviet Union on J. Edgar Hoover's shit list. There were some in the Agency who would have argued it was probably closer to a tie.

The TVs and the radios continued to sound throughout SRD. They were joined now by the noises of Teletype machines, typewriters, telephones, file cabinets closing, shouts, footsteps, sighs.

It went on all afternoon as Charlie, Bruce and their colleagues kept their eyes and their minds switching back and forth from the sound and pictures of the television to the photographs, Photostats, individual pieces of paper, stacks of pieces of paper, cables and other things that were brought in by clerks. The TV brought them this man Oswald at the Dallas police station, the movie theater where he was arrested, what various Dallas officials said about him and what people throughout the nation and the world were saying about the man he allegedly killed, John F. Kennedy.

People came through the area and took orders for dinner. Bruce asked for a pastrami sandwich on an onion roll with mustard and a dill pickle. Charlie ordered a pizza with everything except anchovies. Neither knew—nor cared—where the food was coming from. They weren't asked for money so they assumed it was on the government of the United States of America.

It was just after eight P.M. that Charlie and Bruce each got the summons that would throw them together for the rest of their lives.

"Hancock wants you in his office with your coat on, your tie up," said Jimmy Jackson to Bruce.

"Put your suit coat on and go to Tim's office," was the way Morehead said it to Charlie.

"We're going to the director's office," said Hancock to the two of them a few minutes later. "Do you two know each other?"

Bruce and Charlie, who were standing in front of Hancock's desk, turned to each other and shook hands.

"Mark here," said Bruce.

"I'm George," said Charlie.

Neither ever used their real names to anyone except their immediate supervisors and members of their own families, most of whom didn't even know what they really did for a living.

———

Bruce and Charlie had each been inside the director's office on the seventh floor only once: to receive their respective Blue Hearts. On the way up now in the elevator Bruce asked Hancock: "What's up?"

"You'll know in a minute," said Hancock.

"Good news or bad news?" Charlie asked.

"You'll know in a minute," said Hancock.

Charlie and Bruce exchanged friendly glances of fear.

Who is this guy? Charlie wondered, looking at Bruce. Ivy League, no doubt. Rich, no doubt. Good? Good as me? Good enough? For what?

Why the two of us? thought Bruce. I don't know this George. Midwesterner obviously. Jock probably. Can he hack it? Hack what?

Charlie's mind raced through a wide range of options. Oswald was a CIA asset and this other guy and I are now going to have to do something about it. Like what? No. Impossible. Maybe there are other members of the plot. We will be given the assignment of finding them. It can't be a disciplinary thing. I never heard of Lee

Harvey Oswald. If he did something wrong it wasn't on my string. Unless I did and didn't know it. That's certainly possible.

Bruce also wondered if he had at some time come across Oswald and not realized it. Was there some connection between Oswald and any of the agents or assets he had run? He wondered if somehow he had made a mistake for which he was now going to be ruined. Or maybe there was some kind of special mission he and this George guy were going to be given. To parachute into Moscow, maybe? Sure. Why not? That might be fun.

They followed Hancock right in. There was only one other person in the room besides the director. He was Leo Spivey, the deputy director for plans, who oversaw all Agency covert operations. Both Charlie and Bruce had met Spivey before, although they did not really know him. But among covert operators he was known and respected as a kind of role model/hero, a spymaster of the first order who always played and stayed cool. He, like Hancock, had come to the Agency at its 1947 beginning from the OSS.

Spivey welcomed all three and then turned to present them to John McCone, successor to Allen Dulles, who resigned after the fiasco at the Bay of Pigs. President Kennedy had chosen McCone, a man he barely knew, as Dulles's successor mainly because he was a Republican and that meant cover from the inevitable who-lost-the-Bay-of-Pigs inquiries. McCone also had a reputation for business organization and management that Kennedy thought the Agency sorely needed. McCone had already proved he could keep secrets as head of the Atomic Energy Commission. He made millions in engineering and ship construction before and in between jobs in government. He was now sixty-one years old and, to Bruce's eye, meeting him for the first time, bore a striking resemblance to Allen Dulles. His hair was almost white and it was thinning. He wore rimless glasses and spoke softly and firmly.

"Gentlemen," he said, shaking Charlie's and then Bruce's and then Hancock's right hands. No names were mentioned. McCone probably did not know their real names. Spivey might not have even known them. If McCone remembered he had presented him a Blue Heart just four weeks ago he made no sign of it to Charlie. Dulles had given Bruce his Blue Heart.

McCone guided them toward a set of couches over by the windows. The office was huge and well furnished with heavy dark furniture and heavy books of photographs from California, McCone's native state, where he still had homes as well as personal and financial ties. Bruce and Charlie sat down on one couch; McCone sat across a glass coffee table that was ten feet wide on the other. Spivey and Hancock took chairs at either end of the conversation area.

"I will get right to the point, gentlemen," he said to Bruce and Charlie. "But before I do let me emphasize something that applies to everything you do already but particularly to what I am about to assign you to do. And that, gentlemen, is secrecy. I won't even pause for your response because I know there is no need to receive it because I know what it is."

John McCone sighed and kept talking.

"I have just come from seeing the president. President Johnson, of course."

Of course. Bruce thought he noticed some hesitation in McCone's saying "President Johnson." It did not fall easily from this man's tongue. It did not fall easily from anyone's tongue at this moment. It was still too early, the tragic death of John Kennedy was still too fresh. Kennedy was the president of the United States. Johnson was the vice-president.

Although they did not know it, Charlie and Bruce shared similar opinions of Kennedy. They both liked his style and most of his politics but neither had much time or opportunity in their faraway assignments to form very many solid or informed opinions about him. Josh Bennett had complained passionately to Charlie one night over drinks in Berlin about Kennedy's cowboy attitude toward Vietnam. Josh was afraid it could lead to a major war. An Afghan hand had passed on some rumors just three days ago to Bruce about some FBI wiretaps that had picked up some kind of connection between John Kennedy and Marilyn Monroe.

Charlie thought he detected a slight reddening in McCone's face. Was he embarrassed that he thought it necessary to explain which president he meant? Or was he embarrassed over having to remind himself that Lyndon Baines Johnson was now president of the United States?

McCone said: "We spoke alone in his vice-presidential office at the Old Executive Office Building. As you know, he and the official party arrived back from Dallas not long ago. We spoke in private, just the two of us. He said to me: 'McCone, they tell me the man who killed Jack was a Communist. I want to know if he was ordered by the Russians to do the killing.' He said Edgar—Edgar Hoover of the FBI—told him early information showed that Oswald was a nut who acted alone. I told him that our Agency had no information that would fly in the face of that. He said he assumed that but he had trouble swallowing it. Mr. Johnson said the thing did not smell right. He said he understood that no one could be sure of anything right now but he needed to know within twelve hours what our best conclusion was. He said if the Russians were behind the assassination of President Kennedy then 'I have to get this country ready for war.' That's a quote, gentlemen. 'I have to get this country ready for war.' Maybe not tomorrow, said the president, but soon. 'If the Russians did this we cannot let them get away with it. We have to bomb their red asses into red dust.' End quote, again. I am being this specific because I think it is important that you understand the full implications and significance of the assignment I am about to give you. He said he wanted me back in his office twelve hours from then with the best assessment I could give him of the likelihood of direct Soviet government involvement. I told him, 'Yes, sir,' and I, of course, will do just that. Would anyone like something to drink?"

Charlie and Bruce shook their heads. Spivey said, "No thank you, sir." Hancock said, "I'll pass, too, sir."

Charlie was impressed by a man who could speak in one breath of bombing red asses into red dust and then offer drinks all around ever so calmly and politely. Kennedy had made a good choice in Mr. McCone.

McCone continued: "So, how do we go about giving President Johnson what he needs in twelve hours? How do we give him something that we all can live with, something that will make sense to history as well as the crucial present?"

Charlie felt the breath go out of his entire body.

Bruce tasted the inside of his mouth as it went sour.

"Leo and I and some others have discussed how to go about it and we have come up with a system in which the two of you will play a most pivotal role. Some might suggest the most pivotal role of all. You were identified and chosen and you are here now because of our need for two members of the Soviet Russia Division who are sharp, quick, informed but not bogged down in the world of heavy analysis. Heavy Soviet analyzers would never be able to draw the kind of conclusions we need in twelve hours. We thought two men from the covert-action side who are used to dealing with the KGB and other elements of the Other Side at the operational level might be in a better position to do so and, frankly, would be more temperamentally suited to do so. Do either of you quarrel with that?"

"No, sir," Charlie said. Shit! he thought.

"No, sir," Bruce said. Jesus H. Christ! he thought.

"This does not mean that the normal functions of all other divisions will cease. Your role will be supernumerary in addition to what else is being done. I found in private business that it sometimes helped to bring in fresh perspective from the outside. That is in effect what you two will be doing. Others will also be drawing conclusions and arriving at recommendations. Yours will be matched with them, of course. Do you follow me?"

Charlie and Bruce nodded.

McCone went on: "I am fully aware that a statement of certainty either way is not only unlikely, it is probably impossible. I will be expecting something along the lines of, say, the chances of the

Russians being behind this are sixty-forty because of the following. Or twenty-eighty. Or zero. Or whatever. I think it goes without saying, the more certainty you could put with the assessment the better. Sixty-forty, for instance, is helpful but not enough to warm up bombers or enough to stand them down. Do either of you have any questions?"

Neither Bruce nor Charlie said anything. So McCone stood. And then so did Charlie, Bruce, Spivey and Hancock.

"I, of course, leave the details of how you operate to all of you," said McCone. "I have given instructions that you are to be afforded for the next twelve hours every resource—technical, physical, human and intellectual—that is available to this agency. You are for the next twelve hours cleared for everything we have. If you run across someone who did not get the word, refer them directly to me. A good organization is only as good as its organization. Good luck."

He looked at his wristwatch. "The president said twelve hours. That would mean seven-thirty A.M. for me to see him. That means I will see you here at six-thirty in the morning."

The director extended his right hand to Charlie, who took it and shook it. It was repeated with Bruce.

Hancock moved first toward the door. Charlie and Bruce fell in behind him. Spivey brought up the rear.

And suddenly they were out in a quiet hallway at the elevator.

———————

By the time they got back down to the fourth floor a large conference room had been prepared for them. It was the most secure in the Division area, meaning it was an interior room with no outside windows and with walls that were completely sound-proof. Everything was cleared out except for a long conference table. Three telephones, three small TV sets and a radio were placed on the table along with a supply of legal pads, ballpoint pens, paper clips and similar stationery items.

Spivey had left them at the elevator. Hancock came to the door of the conference room. He said: "All right, how do you want to proceed?"

Bruce and Charlie looked at each other. Charlie said to Bruce: "I think we should take a few private minutes right now to decide that."

"Agreed," Bruce said. Then to Hancock, "We're going to need to begin with two copies of everything that has come in so far."

"Right," Charlie said. "And a list of all human assets in the building and everywhere that we might talk to."

"Sure," Hancock said. His face was grim, tight. He clearly did not enjoy being ordered around by two of his own junior officers. But he left.

Bruce and Charlie walked on into the room and closed the door behind them.

They went to the long table and sat down across from each other at one end.

Charlie said: "I never thought anything like this would ever, ever, ever happen to me."

"Neither did I," Bruce said.

"Hey, fellas, go away and figure out if we should bomb Moscow . . ."

"And start World War Three, a war unlike any ever fought before . . ."

"Where everybody dies, everybody."

"I suggest we begin by putting on the table now any theories, prejudices or ideas each of us may have," said Bruce.

"Good idea," said Charlie. "I'll go first. I think this whole thing is bullshit. If the Soviets were going to kill Kennedy they sure as hell would not use some crackpot defector who would take it to them right off the bat."

"Amen," said Bruce. "They'd farm it out to the Mafia."

"Or the Cubans."

"Which kind? The pro-Castros or the anti-Castros?"

"Each and both," said Charlie.

"So this should be easy for us, right?" Bruce said.

"Sure, easy. Nothing to it. Why us?"

"We're clean minds."

"Sure, clean minds. All right, how do we do it?"

Charlie realized that this guy Mark, whatever else, was quick. But it was still early.

At least George is not an idiot, thought Bruce about Charlie. What else there is about him we shall soon be seeing.

"I suggest that we see ourselves as one," Bruce said.

"What does that mean?"

"It means that both of us read everything, talk to everybody. No compartmentalization here. We both do everything, so when the time comes to reach The Great Conclusion, we come at it with the same information in our respective clean and brilliant heads."

"It's a deal. Let's break everything as we go into two simple categories—Yes and No."

"Explain, please."

"Yes, it tends to indicate the Russkies were behind it. No, it does not. Two stacks, two piles of shit. One at one end of this long table, the other at the other end."

"What if we don't see it the same way? A piece of information comes in, an NSC intercept from Moscow, say. You think it's a No, I think it's a Yes."

"We put it in the middle of the table in a Maybe stack of shit pile," said Charlie. "Why us?"

"Are we ready?" Bruce asked.

"One more question. Do you smoke cigars?"

"No."

"I do when I'm nervous and tired. Can you live with it?"

"For twelve hours I can live with anything."

Charlie glanced at his watch. "We're down to ten hours and eleven minutes already."

They stood. Bruce walked over and opened the door to the hallway. Several people were standing outside holding files and papers and all kinds of other things, waiting for the signal to bring them inside.

Bruce and Charlie got their first jolt ten minutes after they began. It came from reading an internal CIA document dated September 23, 1963. It was from the CIA station chief in Mexico City. It said Lee Harvey Oswald met there on that date with Valery Vladimirovich Kostikov, a consul in the Soviet embassy in Mexico City. The CIA memorandum said Kostikov was also "known to be a staff officer of the KGB. He is connected with the Thirteenth, or 'liquid affairs,' Department, whose responsibilities include assassination and sabotage."

Bruce read it first. Then Charlie, who read the pertinent parts outloud. Across the bottom of the document was a note: "Surveillance photo to follow."

"Well, shit," said Charlie.

"Amen," said Bruce.

They asked for an immediate readout on everything known about Kostikov and told the CIA operator to get the Mexico City station chief on the phone as soon as possible.

And they put the memo in the Yes stack on the table.

Less than a minute later they were on separate phones on the same connection with the CIA station chief in Mexico City.

"What did Oswald and Kostikov talk about?" Bruce asked.

"Oswald wanted a visa to go back to the Soviet Union."

"How do you know that?" Charlie asked.

There was no answer.

"Answer the damned question!" Bruce said. "Or would you rather tell it to the director?"

Charlie smiled and winked at Bruce from across the table.

"We have surveillance in there."

"Where?"

"In the embassy."

"Is the coverage complete?"

"No. Just one office."

"So they could have talked about something else somewhere else?"

"Sure. It was his third visit to the embassy in three days."

"What happened during the other two?" Charlie asked.

"We're not sure."

"Did he see Kostikov?"

"Probably, but we can't confirm."

"What's the photo you wrote about."

"We have a camera taking pictures of everybody who goes in and out. We assumed we had one of this Oswald. Wrong. We missed him."

"How could you get him on the tape but not on camera?" asked Bruce.

"Don't know."

Charlie gave Bruce a hand signal to cut. Bruce nodded and said into the phone: "Stay close. We may be back."

"Get that tape on a plane up here fast," Charlie added.

"What tape?"

"Of Oswald and Kostikov."

"It's already at Langley."

"Thanks."

And they hung up.

They found a file on Oswald's trip to Mexico City. There were brief write-ups on the other two visits to the Soviet embassy plus lengthy reports on similar stops Oswald made at the Cuban embassy in Mexico City. He wanted a visa to go to Cuba, where he would then go on to the Soviet Union. He made quite a scene and the report was full of detail, apparently gleaned from either human or electronic sources within the Cuban embassy.

A clerk brought in a Teletype that listed all the items the Dallas police had found in Oswald's pockets when they arrested him.

Bruce read it first and circled four of the eighteen items on the list. Two membership cards in the pro-Castro Fair Play for Cuba Committee, a piece of paper with two addresses for *The Worker* in New York and another that the police said was "A slip of paper marked Embassy USSR, 1609 Decatur St. N.W., Washington, D.C. Consular Pezhuyehko."

Charlie looked at it and said, "I need a cigar."

"Not yet," said Bruce. "We've just begun."

———

Then came one for the No file. Tim Hancock thought it was so important he brought it in himself.

"What I have here is the report of our man who just debriefed Stone," Hancock said. "That's our name for Anatoli Golitsin, a KGB man who came over to us in Helsinki last year. We've got him situated outside Washington now."

He handed Bruce and Charlie each a copy of the same three pieces of paper.

Bruce and Charlie read together but silently. The pertinent sentences were:

STONE has never heard of Oswald or his wife Marina. He says it is unlikely if not impossible to believe the Soviet Union would mount an assassination hit on President Kennedy. What would be the reason? What would be the reason? he said over and over . . .

He said if by chance some fools in the KGB for whatever reason did decide to take out Kennedy they would never have used a man like Oswald. Too easy to trace right to the Soviet Union. They would have used some Japanese woman or Canadian rock singer before they would have used a defector like Oswald . . .

It is a false trail, STONE said. Look under the Cuban bush. Now there is where something might be found. They are crazy and unreliable. Again, he said this over and over . . .

STONE seemed agitated over the very idea that the Soviet Union was connected with the assassination. He said it was not the way the Soviets would handle a problem. He said look elsewhere. What about the Vietnamese? he asked. Wouldn't they want to get Kennedy for letting the CIA kill Diem?

Bruce finished reading before Charlie. "What are this guy's bona fides?" Bruce asked Hancock.

"Well, he hasn't told us any known lies yet, but he's only been with us six months," Hancock said.

"He couldn't be a plant, could he?" Charlie, who now had finished, asked.

"Ask Angleton."

"Meaning?"

"Meaning we are not of one mind on this at this point."

Charlie said to Bruce: "I think before this little project of ours is over we would probably do well to have a chat with Mr. Angleton. What do you think?"

"Amen."

"I'll arrange it," said Hancock. "Or at least I will try. I may have to get the director or maybe even God in heaven to give him a written order to do so."

Hancock had a final oral report point.

"We can't find Khrushchev."

"Is that important?" Bruce asked.

"We have an eye on him always, twenty-four hours a day wherever he is. He's disappeared. It's never happened before."

"Maybe he's afraid there's a Chinese plot to wipe out some

leaders," Bruce said. "Kennedy was first. He's afraid he's second."

"Anything's possible," Hancock said. "I'm just telling you we've lost him for the first time ever."

Charlie and Bruce were alone again.

"It could also mean Khrushchev knew he damned well better hide because Moscow might soon be in the sights of some B-52," Charlie said to Bruce.

"I hear you, George," Bruce replied.

They turned their attention to Oswald's CIA 201 file, the basic file the Agency keeps on every individual who comes to their official attention. There had been one on Oswald since he defected to the Soviet Union in 1959. The file was thin and consisted mostly of newspaper clippings and reports from CIA personnel in the Soviet Union and a few documents from the Defense and State departments and the FBI. In an overview way the story was there, and Charlie and Bruce each took their time reading and absorbing it.

Lee Harvey Oswald was born in New Orleans on October 18, 1939. His family moved back and forth from there to Fort Worth, Texas. He had a mastoidectomy when he was six, the result of chronic nose problems. On October 3, 1956, the FBI intercepted and "covered" a letter he wrote from Fort Worth to the Socialist Party of America in New York. The letter said:

> Dear Sirs:
> I am sixteen years of age and would like more information about your Youth League. I would like to know if there is a branch in my area, how to join, etc.
> I am a Marxist and have been studying Socialist principles for well over fifteen months. I am very interested in your YPSL.

With it was a coupon from a magazine that had a check mark by the box labeled, "I want more information about the Socialist Party."

Oswald joined the marines the very next month. He went to boot camp in San Diego, to basic infantry training at nearby Camp Pendleton and to radar-operator schools in Florida and Mississippi. He ended up with the First Marine Air Wing at Atsugi, Japan. The file had a note after Atsugi that said further information was available in another file.

Charlie picked up the interoffice phone and asked for that file.

He was discharged from the Marine Corps in September 1959, and after only a few days back home in Texas he went on to New Orleans and boarded a freighter for Le Havre, France. He went to London and then to Helsinki, Finland. A CIA "surveillance" report showed he visited the Soviet consulate in Helsinki. The next notation in the 201 file was on the morning of October 31, 1959, when he walked into the United States embassy in Moscow. He went to the consular section, approached a man behind a desk and slammed his passport down in front of the man. The man happened to be Richard E. Snyder, a CIA agent operating under State Department cover as a senior consular officer. Snyder's report was in detail. It said Oswald told him: "I have come to give up my American passport and renounce my citizenship." And he handed him a handwritten note, a copy of which was in the file. It said that he had entered the Soviet Union "for political reasons" and that he affirmed his allegiance to the Union of Soviet Socialist Republics and his intention of becoming a Soviet citizen. Snyder said in his report that he asked Oswald why he was doing this. "I am a Marxist!" Oswald yelled back. When Snyder pressed him on whether he was prepared to serve his new Soviet masters, Oswald, according to Snyder, said he would turn over what information he could from his work as a marine radar operator, including something of "special interest."

Bruce looked up from that part and said to Charlie: "Have you read the U.S. embassy bit yet?"

"I'm just there," Charlie replied.

"Should we talk to Snyder?"

"What do you think?"

"Maybe, I'm not sure."

"Let's make a note and come back to it later."

They continued reading for a few minutes until a clerk brought in the file about Atsugi.

It said that particular marine base was a top-security installation because it was from there that the Agency's U-2 spy planes took off on their photographic reconnaisance missions over the Soviet Union. The CIA facility was located in several buildings four hundred yards away from the marine hangars behind a sign that said JOINT TECHNICAL ADVISORY GROUP.

Charlie and Bruce read it together.

"Why us?" Charlie asked.

"Because our minds are fresh."

"Can I have a cigar?"

"Not yet."

<hr>

The phone buzzed. Charlie picked it up. "George," he said into the receiver. "Mark here," Bruce said into his. It was Hancock. "Both of you know Martinson."

"Right," Bruce said.

"You bet," Charlie said.

Martinson was the Division's number-one expert on the personnel of the KGB. He was a blunt-speaking walking *Who's Who* of the people who ran and operated the Soviet intelligence service. He watched and studied and listened to those people like they were his pet goldfish.

"He's got the word you wanted on Kostikov," Hancock said.

Martinson was physically as rough as his talk. His body resembled a series of sandbags stacked one on top of the other. His blond hair was a straight-up crewcut. His dress was sloppy. He was, in fact, the exact opposite in just about every way from Bruce and Charlie, who each in their own way were pretty close to being perfect specimens of American males in their mid-thirties.

Martinson came into the room, smiled at Bruce and Charlie and sat down at the long table without being asked and without saying a thing. He had a bright green file folder in his right hand which he placed on the table before him and said: "The headline is this: Valery Vladimirovich Kostikov is an asshole. He cheats on his wife, wears his underwear three days in a row before changing and has yet to do anything in his life right. He's in the KGB because his uncle is Khrushchev's second cousin's husband. He's in the Thirteenth because nobody else would take him. He's in Mexico City because nothing ever happens in Mexico City. He drinks too much, smokes too much, eats too much, screws too much, gambles too much. He made piss-poor grades in all levels of school but did manage to learn a little English, which is probably another reason he's in the Thirteenth. His wife is named Katrina, as are the wives of half the KGB. They met in what passes for high school in the small village in Soviet Georgia where they came from. He went on to college, she did not, even though she's ten times smarter than he is. Women get screwed in more ways than one there just like here. Kostikov has botched just about everything he has touched in the KGB. He was in Bern before coming to Mexico City and tried to recruit a woman member of West German intelligence by putting the make on her. She was a lesbian, but she led him on to the moment of conquest and then turned on the lights and the camera. We got copies of the pictures. They're enough to make a porno fanatic barf. He was run out of Switzerland on a well-run Swiss rail. Before that he set up a dead drop for one of their covert agents in London to pick up a listening device. He chose a dead drop that had been active but never used in seven years. M15 had been watching for all of those seven years, though, and picked up the agent, who was operating in London as an Egyptian bank employee. Like I say, he is an asshole. At a convention of assholes he would be elected chairman by acclamation. Any questions?"

"Oswald had at least one meeting with him in Mexico City two months ago," Bruce said.

"Maybe two more," Charlie added.

"If by some chance Oswald was being run by the KGB to kill Kennedy, what would be the odds they would have used Kostikov to do the running?" Bruce finished.

"I'd say about a million to one," Martinson said. "The KGB has its problems but they are not that stupid. I'm telling you guys, sending him to the post office to buy stamps would be a risky assignment for this clown."

Bruce and Charlie looked at each other. Neither had anything more to say.

Martinson said: "There is one piece of proof that Kostikov had nothing to do with it."

Bruce and Charlie leaned forward.

"It succeeded. Kennedy's dead. I can assure you, if Kostikov had had anything at all to do with it, that would not have been the case. Everybody in the car but Kennedy would have gotten it."

"Thanks," Bruce said.

Martinson closed his file and stood. "Up the Kostikov tree do not bark, my friends," he said.

"Arf, arf," Charlie said.

"He's under a lot of strain," Bruce said to Martinson, who then left after firing a parting shot.

"I keep telling everybody around here that the KGB is a collection of misfits running the only organization in the world that would make the U.S. Post Office look smart, lean and efficient. Nobody listens. Nobody ever goddamn listens. Nobody, including probably you two smart-ass Ivy League warriors."

"We're listening," Bruce said.

"Listen carefully," Charlie said. "Listen carefully and you can hear the sound of our listening. *Whrrr, whrrr.* Ivy League, *kurpluck, kurpluck,* Ivy League, *kurpluck, kurpluck* . . ."

"He's under a lot of strain," Bruce said.

———————

They resumed looking at the 201 and other data that had come in on Oswald's time in the Soviet Union.

After a while Charlie said to Bruce: "Minsk. Why did the sonofabitch go to Minsk? It's four hundred fifty miles from Moscow."

"Did you see the line about the Foreign Language Institute?" Bruce asked.

"Yep."

"And the one after that?"

"Yep," Charlie said, and he read that line aloud. " 'We have a report that an advanced KGB intelligence and espionage school is located next to the Foreign Language School in Minsk. Unable to confirm.' "

Bruce reached for the phone and buzzed Hancock.

"Is there or is there not a KGB dirty school in Minsk?" he said.

"Don't know."

"How can we not know something like that?"

Hancock waited a second before he said: "Back off, Mark."

"Yes, sir."

"What did he say?" Charlie asked.

"He said I should back off."

Charlie picked up the phone to Hancock.

"Sir, this is George. Mark and I are hungry. Could you put somebody on to take our orders or would you like to do it yourself?"

"What do you want?" Hancock said.

"Mark, what would you like to eat?" Charlie said to Bruce.

"A chicken salad sandwich on toasted wheat bread with the

crust trimmed off, plus some rippled potato chips and a Tab,"
Bruce said.

Charlie repeated that into the phone and added: "And for me,
I would like a cheeseburger with fried onions, dill pickle chips,
mayonnaise, a bag of Fritos, and a Budweiser."

Bruce looked up, then resumed reading.

"No drinking in the building," Hancock said.

"Ask the director," Charlie said.

Hancock hung up.

Bruce and Charlie went back to reading.

They came to some difficult parts about Oswald's meeting and
marrying his Russian wife, Marina. There was a July 1961 memo
from a nameless Soviet Russia Division analyst that said:

> We should be alert to the possibility that there may be an
> intelligence interest in the fact of this marriage. We have
> noted a pattern of Soviet women marrying foreigners, being
> permitted to leave the USSR, then divorcing their spouses
> and settling down abroad without returning home. There
> may be reason to explore whether some of these women have
> KGB assignments either alone or in conjunction with their
> spouses. We are looking into several specific instances. The
> most recent and the most telling is the case of Joseph Lewis
> Rhorbaugh.

Attached to that statement with a paper clip was a summary of
the Rhorbaugh matter. Rhorbaugh was an American diamond
merchant who confessed to being a Soviet courier. He told the FBI
and the CIA in his confession that the KGB once tried to get him
to marry a Soviet woman whom they wished to place in Washington, D.C., as an agent. Rhorbaugh refused because he didn't like
the woman and he didn't want to live in Washington.

"Chow call," said a young man in a dark suit as he came through
the door.

He carefully laid out the food for Charlie and Bruce at the other
end of the table. Then he grinned, waved and left. He was barely

out the door before Charlie and Bruce were up, moved and seated in front of their respective orders.

Bruce watched Charlie pour a third of the beer into the glass. "You're not really going to drink that, are you?" Bruce said. "I thought you ordered it just to harass Tim a bit."

"You thought wrong."

"I don't think you should drink that."

"Well, that's too bad. It helps me think."

"Booze doesn't help anybody think."

"Mind your own goddamn business, Mark."

"This is my goddamn business, George. We are talking about bombing Moscow!"

"We are talking here about having a beer! Ease off!"

"You an alcoholic? Got to have it, is that it?"

Charlie slammed the Budweiser bottle down hard on the table and leaped to his feet. "I don't have to take that kind of shit from you, Buster Brown."

Bruce stood. "Oh, yes you do. You take one sip of that beer and I call the director and say forget it. I will not do something as important as this with some asshole with a beer bottle in his goddamn mouth."

"Hancock knows about it! He had it brought to me!"

"I do not give a shit what Hancock thinks. It's what I think that matters and I say no drinking."

"Fuck you!"

And there in the doorway stood Hancock. He was smiling. What had he heard? Nothing, obviously, until he opened the door. The room was soundproof after all. Whatever he heard, he chose to ignore it. He said only: "I'm bringing in a hot one. I told him to come here before he writes it down."

Neither Bruce nor Charlie had a chance to say anything before a man about their age in a sport shirt and slacks came in. He wore thick glasses and his black hair long. He had in his hands a small portable tape recorder.

"He can and will speak for himself," Hancock said. He gave them both a hearty salute and left.

"I'm from technical services," said the man. "I have the proceeds of an electronic surveillance. I was told to bring it here and play it for you even before it was given to secretarial services for a transcript to be made. The voices you are about to hear are those of an FBI agent and an official of the United Nations in New York who is a Russian. Are you ready?"

"That's all you're going to tell us?" Charlie asked.

"That is all I know," said the man from technical services.

They all sat down and listened to the tape. There was no trouble telling who was talking. One of the speakers, clearly the FBI agent, spoke in a southern United States accent. Here's what was said:

FBI: YOU HAVE HEARD ABOUT THE KENNEDY ASSASSINATION?

RUSSIAN: I HAVE. I AM SO UPSET. EVERYONE HERE IS UPSET.

FBI: THE KILLER WAS A COMMUNIST. TIES MAYBE TO THE KGB. DOES THAT MAKE SENSE?

RUSSIAN: NO! NO! IT CANNOT BE.

FBI: WHY NOT?

RUSSIAN: SENSE. IT MAKE NONE. NO. I WOULD KNOW.

FBI: YOU WOULD KNOW WHAT?

RUSSIAN: IF KGB PUT SHOT ON KENNEDY. I WOULD KNOW.

FBI: WHAT'S YOUR THEORY, THEN?

RUSSIAN: NUT. THE MAN IS NUT. BY HIMSELF. NO YOU WORRY. TELL AMERICANS NO TO WORRY. HE IS NUT.

FBI: HAVE YOU EVER HEARD OF OSWALD? LEE HARVEY OSWALD?

RUSSIAN: NO. NO EVER HEARD. EVER.

FBI: ARE YOU SURE?

RUSSIAN: I AM SURE. HE IS NUT. I PROMISE YOU HE IS NUT. I WOULD KNOW.

FBI: THANKS.

RUSSIAN: YOU ARE SO WELCOME.

FBI: TILL WE MEET AGAIN.

RUSSIAN: YAH.

"That's it," said the tech-services man. He stopped the tape, rewound it and left the room.

Bruce and Charlie said nothing but moved back to the other end of the room and picked up their respective phones. Charlie buzzed Hancock.

"Okay, what was it?" Charlie said.

"Surveillance of an FBI agent talking to a KGB man operating undercover at the U.N. He's an FBI asset, has been for months. His code name is 'Top Hat.' Tells them all kinds of things about missiles and personalities. The famous Mr. J. Edgar Hoover doesn't know we know."

"You mean we are bugging the FBI debriefing one of its assets without the FBI knowing it?" Bruce asked.

"You got it."

Charlie whistled.

"How credible is the Russian?" Bruce asked.

"We don't know yet," Hancock said. "There hasn't been enough time to check him out. Angleton's got some doubts. But he always has some doubts."

"How are we coming on our interview with the great man?" Charlie asked.

"It's coming. He said he was too busy now. He would call us when he had time."

"I love him," Charlie said.

"Has Nikita K. turned up?" Bruce asked.

"Not yet," Hancock replied.

Bruce and Charlie went back to their reading. Neither said a word about or made a move toward the other end of the table, where their food was getting stale and cold and Charlie's beer was getting hot.

They dug into the growing collection of material about Oswald's ties and actions and beliefs about Cuba. There were police reports from New Orleans about his arrest for illegally distributing pro-Castro material on a street corner and surveillance reports from the New Orleans police and the FBI about that and other activities. There was a written transcript of a radio debate Oswald was in about Cuba, a Photostat of a post-office slip that showed that Oswald rented a post-office box in Dallas in the name of the Fair Play for Cuba Committee and the American Civil Liberties Union, interviews with "sources" who were present at meetings when Oswald said he loved Cuba and "hated America," copies of letters he had written to people saying similar things as well as others that had been sent to various Cuban offices and officials at the United Nations and elsewhere.

The only thing that aroused the special interest of both Charlie and Bruce was the fact that Oswald was quoted at least twice as telling people he thought "the CIA was trying to kill Castro."

"Let's ask somebody about that," Charlie said to Bruce.

"Good luck on our getting an answer," Bruce said. "But, I agree, let's ask."

Charlie buzzed Hancock. "Question, Tim," he said. "Are we trying to assassinate Castro?"

"Goodness gracious, no," Hancock said. "We're not in that line of work."

"We don't mean our division, we mean our agency, our country," Bruce said.

"Okay, then," Hancock said. "My answer is—not that I know of, gentlemen. It is possible that the Army Corps of Engineers or the U.S. Department of Agriculture or the Federal Deposit Insurance Corporation has put out a contract on Fidel Castro, but I doubt it."

Bruce said: "We hereby request that you scrub the Agency for people and files on possible assassination attempts on Castro."

"Sure," Hancock said. "It'll take thirty or forty seconds to round it up. Why don't the two of you hold your breath till it arrives there on your beautiful long table?"

"Seriously, Tim," Charlie said. "If we were trying to kill him and Castro knew about it, wouldn't that be a pretty good motive for a preemptive strike against Kennedy?"

"Give us your best educated guess," Bruce added.

"We do not assassinate people. Period. Turn the page. Forget it."

He hung up.

Bruce said to Charlie: "What's your best guess?"

"I don't have one," Charlie said.

They resumed their reading about Oswald and the Fair Play for Cuba Committee.

After a while Charlie said: "I think it all goes in the No stack. Somewhere in there may be some kind of Oswald tie with Cuba, but it says zero about a Soviet connection."

"I agree," Bruce said. "If it means bombing Havana, then that's somebody else's problem."

They put their respective files and papers in the No section of the table.

"Let's look at the stuff about the redefection," Bruce said.

"Why not?" Charlie responded.

The phones rang. Charlie got to his first.

"There is a personal emergency call for Mark," said Hancock. "Does he want it?"

Bruce/Mark was on the line now. "Sure. Who is it from?"

"The guy said he was your brother. Do you have one?"

"I do," Bruce said.

Charlie waved at Bruce and said: "I'll give you some privacy. I need to make a head call anyhow. I hope it's not bad news."

Bruce said, "Thanks."

A couple of beats after the door closed Bruce heard the voice of his brother Duane.

"Buddy? This is Duane." Buddy had been Bruce's nickname from the day he was born. It was given to him by Duane, who was ten years old at the time, and it stuck.

"Hi, Duane," said Bruce. "What's happened? Are Mom and Dad all right?"

"Mom's got a cold and Dad misses getting *The New York Times* every day but they're fine," Duane said. "I talked to them yester-day. You should call them. They wondered why you hadn't. I didn't tell them you were in the country." Mildred and Jonathan Clark, Duane and Bruce's parents, had recently moved from Greenwich, Connecticut, to a large condominium in Scottsdale, Arizona. Mr. Clark was a retired senior partner of Salomon Broth-ers, a major New York investment-banking firm.

"Why have you called me?" Bruce said. "This is a very busy time for me."

"Sure, sure. I understand." Bruce heard something in his big brother's voice that he had heard only a few times before. Dread. Fear. Panic. Terror. "Bud, a man came with the other half of the card."

"Jesus, no," Bruce said. The words came not just from his mouth but from inside his entire body.

"He came right to my office here at the college. Just walked in and put the card on my desk."

"What did he want?"

"He wanted me to call you. He wanted me to give you a message. He knew you worked where you work."

"How did he know that? Nobody's supposed to know that!"

"He didn't say how he knew. I didn't ask him. He just knew it."

Duane Rollins Clark's voice was now shaking like a row of water glasses on a new waiter's tray.

"I don't want the message," Bruce said. "I'm going to hang up."

"Bud, listen. He said to tell you they had nothing to do with it."

"With what, for Christ's sake?"

"He didn't say. But he said that was the truth and I should tell you so you could tell everyone else who should know."

Bruce had been careful with his words, but Duane had been, too. Good work, brother. An eavesdropper would not have heard much that would do damage. The word was that calls in and out of Langley were sometimes monitored by security and/or CI, but that kind of routine make-work was unlikely to be happening now because of the Kennedy assassination. Even so, Bruce said to Duane and any Agency eavesdropper: "Tell him that I got out of the insurance business a long time ago and I do not think you should pay any attention to shakedown hoods with grudges about old debts."

"What are you talking about, Bud?"

"Good-bye, Duane. I'll call Mom and Dad."

―――――――――

Charlie had gone first to the men's room down the hall and then had circled back by Hancock's office.

"You still keep cigars around?" he asked Hancock.

"For you, Mr. Master Spy, of course," said Hancock. He pulled a box of cigars out of a desk drawer and let Charlie help himself to one. Without being invited, Charlie sat down in the chair across from the desk.

"This wasn't your idea, was it?" he asked Hancock.

"What?"

"Us. Me and Mark or whoever he is."

"You want the truth, I suppose. The truth is no. Goddamn, no. It was the director's idea. He said it was a technique he picked up in 'the private sector.' You know the private sector. That's where people screw other people for money. At least here in the public sector we do it for the national interest. He said the technique is called 'outside-inside.' Take people from the inside and put them in an outside role. Checks and balances and all of that. Fresh views and all of that. Bullshit and all of that. I could have answered his question without looking at one thing."

"What question?"

"The question, asshole. Were the Soviets behind Oswald and the assassination?"

"Your answer, sir?"

"No. And I assume that is the one you two geniuses will come up with, too."

"No comment. The geniuses are still at work."

"Speaking of that, why don't you get your butt out of here and get back to it?"

"Question?"

"Yes, sir?"

"Do we have any assets in the Kremlin we could tap on this? If it was a Soviet deal it would have had to be ordered from the very top."

"No."

"No what?"

"No, we have no assets in the Kremlin."

"I hope to hell you are lying."

"Get out of here."

Charlie put the unlit cigar between the forefinger and index finger of his right hand.

"How do we keep an eye on Khrushchev if we don't have somebody inside?" he said.

"You don't need to know that," Hancock said.

"I need to know everything."

"I define everything. Good-bye."

———————————

Charlie held up the cigar to Bruce. "What about it? What if I stay at this end of the table?"

"Go ahead," Bruce said. Suddenly the smell of cigar smoke seemed like a trivial problem in his life.

Charlie lit the cigar and blew the smoke straight up in the air above his head. He tossed the spent wooden match he had used onto the plate with the chicken salad sandwich.

"We forgot to eat," he said to Bruce.

"Right," Bruce said.

"Did your brother have some bad news?"

"No, no. Some financial problem he thought was urgent but wasn't."

Charlie took another draw from the cigar.

"You realize we don't know one damned thing about each other?" he said. "That's weird. People sharing a foxhole should know about each other."

Bruce put down the file he was reading. "How good are you at figuring out somebody's life story without being told, just by watching and listening?"

"Pretty good."

"I'll bet you I'm better."

"What'll be the bet?"

"We each go through the other's story. Whoever comes closest to the real one about the other wins. If I win, you put out that goddamn cigar. You win, you keep smoking it."

"Bullshit. I win and I not only keep smoking, which I already am, but I have one sip of that hot piss beer."

"Okay, you first."

Charlie leaned toward Bruce at the other end of the table and said:

"East Coast."

Bruce nodded.

"New England. Probably Connecticut."

"Right."

"Ivy League. Probably Princeton."

"Harvard."

"Jock. Probably basketball."

"Baseball."

"Pitcher."

"First base."

Charlie took another draw on the cigar. "Middle child."

"Youngest child and fuck you."

"Rich."

"Rich."

"Recruited into Agency by a professor."

"Right. Weren't we all?"

"No comment. Your turn."

Bruce said: "Midwest. Missouri. Probably southwest Missouri. Modest income. Scholarship student, Ivy League. Probably Yale. Oldest child. Football player. Tight end or linebacker."

Charlie shook his head and slowly reached across and put out his cigar. "You are amazing, Buster Brown."

"Where does that come from?" Bruce asked.

"What?"

"Buster Brown."

"It's the name of shoes they used to make for little boys in southwest Missouri."

Charlie moved back to his chair across from Bruce at the other end of the table.

"While I was out," he said, "I went by and asked Hancock if we had any assets inside the Kremlin we could ask about whether there was high-level Soviet involvement in this. He said we didn't have any. I don't believe that."

"I do."

"Why?"

"We're not good enough at that yet."

There was a call from Hancock. "Angleton's on his way to see you two geniuses," he said.

Before either had a chance to think about it there he was. James Jesus Angleton in the flesh. In the tall, gray, thin, ghostly flesh. He was wearing a dark blue suit, the only man Bruce and Charlie had seen with his suit coat on since they left the director's office with their special mission. His thick, round glasses gave them each a fast glance. They each rushed to shake his hand and offer him a chair at their table. He took it.

He had nothing in his hands, no notebook, no green file folder, nothing at all.

"I understand your assignment," he said. "I have been asked to reflect on it and I have come to do so."

Charlie, who was sitting right next to him, had no problem hearing. But Bruce, across the table, picked up his chair and moved it around to the end so he would be closer. Angleton, obviously, did not come to speak in an oration voice. Bruce suddenly wondered if he had ever made an oration, a speech. He was known in legendary, heroic terms for his poetry writing and editing at Yale, his orchids, his devotion to Israel and Israeli intelligence and his burning belief that most everyone had, until proven otherwise, to be considered a suspected Soviet mole. This included most of the employees of the Central Intelligence Agency, all of the employees of the State Department and many others throughout the government. Both Charlie and Bruce were, like all Agency people, regularly investigated and fluttered by Angleton's people. Neither, of course, had ever been in the presence of the man himself, much less exchanged a word with him.

Angleton said: "I have looked at everything we have. I have talked to everybody we have. I will not review with you either what I looked at or to whom I talked for the obvious security reasons."

"Sir," Charlie broke in, "as you know we are to have access to everything in this Agency that bears on the central question of the assassination."

Angleton looked through those glasses at Charlie as if he had just yelled "Shit!" in church. Bruce, with a rush of admiration for

"George," concluded that he had just witnessed the first time a lowly Agency person had interrupted James Jesus Angleton.

"If I may continue," Angleton said.

"Of course, sir," Charlie said.

"Since you have raised the question of The Central Question," said Angleton, "let me say that I do not believe the central question is the one you two have been assigned to answer. Was the Soviet Union behind the assassination of President Kennedy? is your question. That is not the central question. The central question is who shot Kennedy and why? Your central question is too narrow. You answer it and all you have is an answer to one question that does not necessarily mean you have the answer to the central question. From your answer leads only other questions, so you end up with no answer at all. No answer that means very much. But since you have been asked to arrive at such an answer and since I have been asked to contribute to your deliberations, let me say a few things to you.

"First, every piece of evidence we have indicates that Lee Harvey Oswald would be the last person the Other Side would have chosen to murder the president of the United States. Common sense and history shows that there are two kinds of political or government-organized and -sanctioned assassinations: open assassinations and closed assassinations. An open assassination is one that is committed publicly by a faction or government in a way designed to bring immediate attention and credit and, hopefully, acclaim to the assassin or assassins and any sponsors they might have. We destroyed this awful tyrant because he was an evil and wicked man for the good of our country, our world, our whatever. The unsuccessful assassination attempts on Adolph Hitler by his military commanders are examples of this type. If they had been successful, the perpetrators would have stepped forward to announce their accomplishment and their complicity with great pride.

"The second type, the closed assassination, is a covert operation. The Labor party of Great Britain decides that the Conservative party prime minister must be eliminated for the good of their country. They decide to mount an assassination attempt on the life of the prime minister. But they realize that there are definite political risks in doing so. The British people might not think that is the way to change leaders of their government. So the Labor people do it secretly in a way designed to forever protect them from being identified as the perpetrators of the terrible deed.

"Let's run the Soviet Union question through those two tests. Why would the Soviets want to commit an open assassination against President Kennedy and thus trigger the beginning of World War Three, a war unlike any other in history, a war that would destroy as many and as much of them as us? It would be geopolitical suicide. So that rules out the possibility that they would intentionally choose an assassin that would automatically and quickly be traced to the doorstep of the Kremlin. It is absurd on the face of it, as I am sure I do not need to tell two seasoned and intelligent Soviet Russia Division officers as yourselves.

"So to the closed assassination. Let's assume for discussion purposes that the Soviets wanted Kennedy dead for some reason but did not want it traced to them. Why would they select someone like Oswald for the task, someone so closely and quickly and unmistakably associated with them?

"There is, of course, a third type of assassination. This is the random assassination. The killing of an important government leader or public figure is done by someone of a demented or strange state of mind. The assassin or assassins do it on their own for their own twisted personal or political reasons. It appears that is the type we are talking about here. That is the direction the evidence points, at least."

Angleton bowed his head slightly, untangled his body and smiled. It was the first time he had smiled since entering the room.

"Of course, there could be another explanation, one that does not fit into any of these three categories. The assassins create a public or covert story—a legend, to use our term—that points to them directly and immediately, as is the case with Oswald. We, the other side, are expected to look at the obviousness of it and conclude that there is no way it could be the Russians because if they wanted to assassinate Kennedy they would not choose such a person to do it. Are you following me, gentlemen?"

Bruce and Charlie nodded.

Angleton said: "The guiding principle for us is simply, the obvious is never the obvious if it's too obvious, or is it?"

Charlie so much wanted to ask him to repeat that. But he held his tongue.

Angleton looked right at Bruce and continued: "The point is that it is certainly possible that I have fallen victim to this very technique. If I have, then they have been successful and I would be the first to congratulate them for their cleverness and their craft. But I do not believe that is the case. I am not certain because I am not certain of anything. What do I know about the two of you, for instance? I looked at your files before coming here now. I know what it says about where you were born, where you were educated, where you have served in this agency and how well you have performed your duties. But is that all there is to know about you? Which one of you had the problem with the Czech defector?"

Charlie raised his right hand.

"The file says you performed courageously. But the operation was blown. Why? Nobody knows why it was blown. Could it be because you are working for the other side? Could it be that you did some little thing wrong, wrong enough to cause the operation not to work? Could it be that in all of our prehiring investigations of you and your background, could it be that in all of our flutters, all of our careful perusal of your activities since joining the Agency, that we missed something? Could it be that there is something in your personality, in your habits, in your history, that makes you vulnerable to blackmail or pressure or money? Could it be, could it be?"

"I was shot, for God's sake!" Charlie said.

"Oh, yes. You have my condolences. But correct me if I'm wrong, it was a wound from which you will fully recover. Maybe the Czech was under strict instructions to shoot you in order to preserve your credibility but in a place that would assure your quick and full recovery in order that you might continue to function for us and thus for them."

"That is absurd," Charlie said. "I very much resent your even suggesting such a thing."

"I can survive your resentment, young man," said Angleton with a smile. "I cannot survive your treachery, if in fact it existed. My point, I believe, is an obvious one." He turned toward Bruce. "I presume you follow my logic and my lesson for the day?"

"I do, yes, sir," Bruce said. "I do."

"I follow the lesson," Charlie said, "but not the point as it applies to our Central Question."

"I have given you my assessment of the situation to the best of my ability. I did it because I was ordered to do so. I personally think it is a poor procedure to put a matter such as this in the hands of two junior covert operators, but that, of course, is not my decision. That said, I did my duty. I do not believe the Soviet Union had anything at all to do with the assassination of President Kennedy. I say that well aware that a development tomorrow or in one hundred years could prove me wrong. I have also fully acknowledged that at this early stage of the investigation it is certainly possible that I have fallen victim to a very clever scheme of disinformation. The Soviets intentionally made it look so obvious that they were behind it that we would, of course, immediately discount such a possibility. The decision on what you tell the director, of course, is yours. I have already said to him what I have just told you. He asked that I also speak to you and I have done so."

He bowed his head again, stood and left the room.

———————

Somebody came in and removed the uneaten trays of food and drink. Somebody else came in a few minutes later and brought a thermos of fresh coffee. Bruce and Charlie talked quietly from time to time about a certain interview or other piece of information. But neither said a word about Angleton. What both had to say had already been said so often by so many, what was the point? What was the point of saying again that James Jesus Angleton was a larger mystery himself than any of those he worked on?

The televisions continued to play with the sound way down, but neither of them paid much attention. They were both into their reading. Occasionally one would get up and walk around the room. Bruce left to go to the head. When he got back, Charlie did. Both avoided routes that would take them near Hancock or anyone else.

The real taskmaster was the clock.

It was Charlie who finally said, "Should we start going through some scenarios?"

Bruce said: "Why not?"

"Are you really as cool as you appear to be?" Charlie asked.

"No. It's a personality defect. I don't show fear."

"I'm out of my mind."

"The redefection. What's your reading?"

"It stinks," Charlie said. "It stinks like week-old garbage in the sunshine."

"Week-old garbage in the sunshine?"

"Mr. Wordsmith, I am." It was said with a smile. "Here is a guy with a love-Russia thing since he was a kid, defects to the Soviet Union, announces his hatred for the good old U.S.A. and promises to turn over everything he knows about being a radar operator at an air base where the U-2 operates. He goes off to live in Minsk, home of a suspected KGB dirty-works school. Picks up a Russian wife . . ."

"Whose uncle is a colonel in Soviet military intelligence," Bruce said.

"I missed that."

"It's a line in one of those reports."

"Okay. This guy then then comes back to Moscow twenty months later and says to our people, 'Forget it. I love America, I'm still an American because I didn't become a Soviet citizen after all, so give me back my passport so I can get the hell out of here and be a good little American ex-marine again.' "

"I pick up the same odor you do."

"Now, what does it mean? Well, it could mean the worst, the obvious worst. He went over as a defector and was sent back as a KGB agent with another agent who is now his wife."

"To kill the president?"

"We'll get to that later."

"There could be another explanation. Do you remember what Hancock told us in his office after he got that call that they had arrested somebody?"

"I sure as hell do. He said, 'He's one of ours.' Something like that."

"Something exactly like that. Let's go see Hancock."

─────────────

Hancock blew his stack.

"You assholes!" was what he said after carefully closing the door to his soundproof office.

"We both heard you say he may be one of ours," Bruce said. "Why did you say that if he wasn't?"

"I meant something else. I meant he was a Division problem because he was a former defector."

"Let me try out a scenario on you," Charlie said.

"Screw your scenarios," Hancock said. "Our Agency would come crushing down around our heads and our asses and stay down there forever if it was ever even suggested the man who shot the president was in any way connected to the Central Intelligence Agency. Cool it, stuff it, screw it, fuck it, shut it up."

"Tim, you have to hear us out," Charlie said.

"I do not. I run this division and I know who works for us and who does not. Lee Harvey Oswald did not work for us. Period. That is all you two need to know. Now, get back into your inner sanctum and wrap things up. Time is almost up anyhow. If you want to destroy this agency go over to the other fucking side."

Charlie and Bruce, without even exchanging a glance, played a duet of silence, a technique that both had been taught in the same CIA training school at Camp Perry, Virginia, down by Williamsburg. The best way to get somebody to talk is to shut up and just look at him, or her. Silence, in the right situation, can be the most intimidating weapon there is. People seem compelled to fill it with something, usually their own words.

Hancock clearly was rattled. He stared back at them for a few seconds and then said, "I said, get out of here. I said, this guy Oswald did not work for us. Sure, he was talked to by our guys at the Moscow embassy. Sure, there was a 201 on him because he was a defector. But that is it."

"What if he was a false defector?" Bruce said. "What if we set him up to defect and then come back as a KGB man but really as one of ours?"

"No way!"

"Did Domestic Contacts talk to him when he came back from the Soviet Union last year?" Charlie asked.

"I don't know," Hancock said. Domestic Contacts, or DC, was a branch of the Agency that interviewed Americans who traveled to the Soviet Union and other Warsaw Pact countries in search of tidbits of information. They were particularly keen on looking at photographs that tourists took while traveling in those countries and talking to scientists who had just returned from conferences attended by Soviet bloc scientists.

"I can't imagine a more obvious thing to do than for DC to sit down with a guy who had just come back from a major defection to the Soviet Union," Charlie said. "I can't imagine a more stupid thing, frankly, than not to."

"Is there a DC man in Dallas?" Bruce asked.

"Yes," Hancock said.

"We want to talk to him," Bruce said.

"Remember what you were asked to do, young warriors of adventure and danger," Hancock said. "The director didn't say one goddamn thing to the two of you about determining if the sonofabitch worked for us."

He reached for a telephone on his desk and said something to somebody. The three of them sat in silence for a few seconds. The phone buzzed. He picked up the receiver, listened for a second and then placed it on a speaker machine.

"I am making it possible for two of our people here in the office with me to ask you a few questions," Hancock said.

"Fine," said a male voice. "Whatever." Charlie liked the sound of the man. He decided he was probably in his late forties or early fifties. He could have even been an old covert man. Many of them went to DC before retirement.

Bruce asked the first question. "Did you interview Oswald since he moved to Dallas?"

"No," said the voice. "In fact, you'll never believe what happened. I was over at the Trade Mart waiting for the president to come to speak. My cover here is as an official of the Army Corps of Engineers. I was there as just a person who had bought a ticket to the luncheon. When I heard about the shooting of the president I rushed back to my office. There, in my In basket from the morning Agency pouch, was a file on Oswald with a request from DC, Langley, that I talk with him. Isn't that something?"

"It sure is," Charlie said. "It's something some people might have trouble believing."

The voice on the phone from Dallas took a breath. He was clearly deciding what to say and his decision was a pure old-salt professional. "So be it," he said. "The truth is always the most difficult for people to believe."

"Where is that Oswald file now?" Bruce asked.

"It's still on my desk."

"Are you sitting there now?"

"I am."

"You've had a long day and night, too. Would you mind opening it and telling us what's in it?"

"No problem," said the man in Dallas.

And there was the sound of paper being moved about. "There's not much here. First, there is a report from Moscow on his defection. It's by one of ours. There's a memo from the Marine Corps about his service and discharge. An FBI report on his activities in New Orleans for the pro-Castro people. A transcript of a radio program he was on. Some paper on a trip he made to Mexico City sixty days ago, some contacts he made with the Soviet and Cuban embassies there."

"That's fine," Bruce said. "It sounds like it's pretty much a duplicate of his 201."

"That's exactly what it is," said the man in Dallas.

"Does it say anywhere in there that he was ever an asset of ours?" Charlie asked.

Hancock shot Charlie the finger.

"Let me see now," said the man in Dallas. Again, there was the sound of moving paper. "No. Nothing like that."

"How about of the FBI?" Bruce asked.

"Nope. Don't you guys have a 201 up there?"

"We do," Charlie said. "Just doing some cross-checking."

"Did you know Oswald was in Dallas before you came back and saw that file?" Bruce asked.

There was a slight pause before the DC man said, "Yes and no. I knew there was a former Soviet defector named Oswald in town. I had picked that up from an FBI source and from some people in the Russian émigré community. I did not know it officially."

"Why didn't you talk to him?" Charlie asked.

"That's not how it works in DC," said the man in Dallas.

Hancock gave Charlie and Bruce a fierce stare. The call was over.

"Thanks a lot," Charlie said.

"No problem," said the man in Dallas.

"Appreciate your help," Bruce said. "One last difficult question."

"Sure."

"Were there any of our people in Dallas besides you?"

"When?"

"Yesterday, today."

"Not that I know of."

"Time to go," Hancock said.

"It is an awful thing that happened," said the man in Dallas. "I liked Kennedy. I went to school with one of his brothers . . ."

It is an awful thing that happened. Yes! My God, yes! Bruce and Charlie looked right at each other. It was something neither had said or even thought about since this all began so many hours ago.

It is an awful thing that happened to President John F. Kennedy in Dallas, Texas.

"Satisfied?" Hancock asked them both after the phone was disconnected.

"Yes and no," Bruce said.

"Fuck you," Hancock said. "We found little Nikita."

"Where?"

"At Spaso House." Spaso House was the United States ambassador's residence in Moscow. "He came in to sign the condolence book and issue a statement of sympathy for the American people."

"Where had he been?" Charlie asked.

"Nobody asked him."

———————

They had their first conversation about what time it was.

"Holy shit," Charlie said. "We've got less than an hour left."

"I know," Bruce said.

They were back in their soundproof room. Somebody had brought in more coffee, plus a jug of orange juice and a basket of croissants.

Neither Bruce nor Charlie did anything but pour themselves more coffee.

"Let's start talking," Charlie said. "About anything each of us might have on his mind and see where we end up. I can't organize what I think. I am not sure what I think. I am sure I do not know what I know."

"We don't know anything," Bruce said.

Charlie lurched forward in his chair. "I've got an idea," he said. "Let's get out of here."

"Oh, come on . . ."

"I mean let's go outside and walk around. It'll clear our heads."

"It's probably cold."

"I doubt if we'd feel it."

They put on their suit coats. Bruce buzzed Hancock. "We're going for a walk outside," he said.

"Don't get lost," Hancock said. "It would reflect badly on the Division for two of its prized covert operators to disappear in the woods of Langley." There was a pause. "By my watch you are now down to forty-eight minutes."

"By ours, too. Thanks."

They rode one of the regular elevators down to the lobby level instead of the back one reserved for covert types and others who needed to keep their faces from being widely seen. It was five in the morning; they did not expect to run into other people. They were wrong. The elevator was jammed when they got on it. Frowning people carrying various colors of files got off and on at every stop on the way down.

A president had been assassinated. If the Soviet Russia Division was up to its eyeballs in work, it stood to reason there would be others in the Agency equally so. Could the Greeks have done it? What about the Vietnamese? The Italians? The South Africans? The Upper Voltans? It was something neither Bruce nor Charlie had considered until they got on the elevator. They assumed that only they were hard at work, only they held the future of the world in their hands and minds.

It was still dark outside and it was cold. But not unbearably so, and without talking about it they headed for the woods on the other side of the main entrance to the huge gray concrete building. That was the direction of the Potomac River, the scene the director and the deputy directors looked out upon from their various offices and suites.

On bright, clear days they could see the steeple of the Washington Cathedral at the corner of Massachusetts and Wisconsin avenues. It was only fitting.

There was a path that went a few yards into the trees, some of which still had some color. Most were already on their way to being brown and on the ground. Again, with no prior discussion, they turned right and walked toward the main gate on the Dolley Madison Boulevard side of the complex. There were streetlights around so there was no problem seeing where they were going, which was nowhere in particular anyhow.

Charlie fished a cigar out of his coat pocket and lit it as they walked.

"Same one?" Bruce asked.

"You bet. I stuck it in my pocket just in case," Charlie said.

It was another thirty or forty seconds before they got down to it. Bruce began.

"It's hard to ignore Angleton's conclusion. It makes absolutely no sense for the Soviets to go for Kennedy, one; it makes no sense to use this Oswald if they did decide to do it, two."

"We knew that and could have said that and we did say that when all of this started nine hours ago. That bothers me."

"What exactly bothers?" asked Bruce.

"That. Angleton's final point. That all of the facts—most of the facts, at least—point right at the Soviets but all of the conclusions point away from them. Is it too obvious? Or what was it the great Mr. Angleton said: What is obvious is not always as obvious as it appears or is it? Something like that. You watch much television?"

"No. They don't have much where I usually am."

"Me neither. But you know about a cop show called *Naked City?*"

"Sure. There are eight million stories and all that crap."

"That's it. Once they had a murder case where a guy who was well known as Billy the Confessor came in and said he did the killing. It was about the seventh or eighth murder this guy had confessed to. Each of those earlier times they asked him a few questions about the details and it was clear he had nothing to do with it. This time when he came in the cops didn't even ask a question. They just waved him off and told the guy to leave them alone. Later on, like forty-three minutes or so as is required on TV, the cops got lucky and something led them to the fact that Billy the Confessor really had killed the guy this time. His earlier confessions were a setup cover to the real killing he planned. A kind of wolf-wolf story in reverse. If it hadn't been a TV show he'd have probably gotten away with it."

"I'm a little uneasy," said Bruce, "using some kind of goddamn TV cops-and-robbers show as a route to solving the assassination of a president of the United States."

"I'd say 'Fuck off, Mark' if I had the time to waste," Charlie said, taking a long draw on his cigar and making no effort this time to avoid some of the smoke going right into Bruce's face. They were walking side by side, with Bruce on the right. The path was a finely crushed gravel. "You got the point, I think, and that is what is important. Sometimes we Missouri hicks follow hick routes and roads to important destinations."

"I do have time to say 'Fuck off, George,' " Bruce said.

The guard post at the gate with its bright lights and several uniformed CIA security police was now only twenty or so yards away. Bruce motioned with his head for them to cross the street and head back toward the building on the sidewalk on the other side. Charlie nodded.

Their pace slowed to a shuffle.

"What were you getting at with the DC man in Dallas?" Charlie asked. "You are not thinking that some of our own killed Kennedy, I hope?"

"No, no," Bruce said. "Just fishing. It occurred to me that there could be some renegades around, some loonies who were pissed about the Bay of Pigs or something. I thought if maybe the DC guy had seen anyone around . . . well, I don't know."

"It's unlikely he would have known them to recognize them if they had been there."

"True. Like I said, just fishing."

They stopped walking and faced each other.

"Okay, what do we tell McCone?" Bruce said. He said it very softly, as if it were more of a statement than a question.

"I'm leaning toward telling him . . . well, that we may be the victims of what Angleton called a gigantic and most incredibly clever disinformation scheme. Maybe the most gigantic and incredibly clever in the history of the glorious business we are in, something on a par with the great Trust ruse." In the early days of the revolution the Bolsheviks created a huge anti-Bolshevik organization called The Trust that they ran and controlled and ultimately used to squelch and destroy all legitimate opposition to their tactics and rule.

"So you think the Russians were behind it?" Bruce asked.

"Don't you?"

"Yes, yes, yes. I think."

"Well said. Yes, yes, yes . . . I think."

Each closed his eyes and lowered his head. Not in prayer but in wonder, at the wonder of what they had just said.

They moved forward another four or five steps in silence. The quiet of the darkness remained. Lights were on in windows all over the huge building, the so-called House that Dulles Built. A hopeful eye could have also picked up the beginning of the day's light in the East, through the trees toward the river.

"Why did they do it?" Charlie asked. "Why did they want Kennedy dead?"

"That we cannot answer in ten hours."

Bruce raised the collar on his coat. Charlie tossed his cigar butt on the sidewalk and slowly, deliberately crushed it.

"What if we're wrong?" Bruce asked.

They turned up the wide sidewalk to the front steps of the building.

"We say, 'Whoops, sorry about that,' " Charlie said.

"When do we say it—before or after the bombs hit Moscow?"

"Let's go back to our room for one last look."

———————

The seconds ticked off like popping hand grenades. It was now 6:18 A.M.

Bruce buttoned his shirt and moved his tie back up against his Adam's apple. Charlie was looking through a small stack of paper, the stuff that had come in while they were outside.

"Anything?" Bruce asked.

"Here's the written report on Khrushchev's magic reappearance. There's nothing in it we didn't already know. That's about it."

Charlie got his tie in place.

"All right now," Bruce said. "What's it going to be? War or peace?"

"What? What do you mean?" Charlie had not really heard Bruce.

"Hey, George," Bruce said. "Our moment has come. We have to decide exactly . . ."

"The time difference between here and Moscow is twelve hours. Right?" Charlie was agitated about something.

"Right."

Charlie grabbed the report off the table. "Look at this!"

Bruce followed Charlie's right forefinger to a place on the paper in front of them. "Khrushchev disappeared from our sight for the first time ever exactly thirty-eight minutes before those shots were fired in Dealey Plaza in Dallas."

It was now 6:22.

Charlie grabbed the phone and called Hancock. "Tell the director we need another 10 minutes."

"No," Hancock said. "Get your asses down here."

Charlie hung up and said to Bruce: "We've got to suck it in, decide what we say. No more time."

"No more time indeed."

"What else can we say except that it adds up to a Soviet plot? Khrushchev disappeared because he knew what was coming. It was their deal."

"With odds?"

"Sure," Charlie said. "I'd say eighty-five—fifteen."

"Seventy–thirty," Bruce said.

"Why?"

"Motive. I don't get why they would want Kennedy dead."

"Could there be some renegade hard-liners who want a war?"

They put their suit coats on and moved toward the door.

"Remember what that creep Martinson said," Bruce said.

"What?"

"That the Soviets are one helluva lot dumber than we give them credit for."

"So?"

"So, to conceive and pull off this so-obvious-it's-not-us routine would take geniuses of high and unprecedented magnitude."

Charlie stopped. "What are you saying to me?"

"I'm saying, wait a minute."

"One minute is about all we now have."

"Do we really want to do this? Do we really want to be the guys who made a small contribution toward the beginning of World War Three? Do we really want to do that?"

"The alternative is to lie. Say, Well, sir, we looked at all of this and we think in all probability—maybe ninety-nine to one—that the Russians had nothing to do with it."

"That is clearly what everyone wants to hear. Why not tell them that so the world can go on about its business?"

"And we go about our business knowing that we think the Russians killed Kennedy and we helped them get away with it?"

"If we are right and they really did do it, they won't get away with it. There is bound to be a massively thorough investigation of the assassination and it will come out. When it does they will have to pay whatever hell they deserve. But this morning? Would we really want the president of the United States to 'start getting the American people ready for war' based on our conclusions? We're guessing, and I mean guessing, that Soviets mounted a disinformation scheme to make it look so obvious that they were behind the assassination that we would believe they weren't, which was exactly what they want us to believe because they really were? If Angleton hadn't planted that twisted little weed in our heads . . ."

Charlie shook his head slightly from left to right like there was a fly in his face. "I told you this whole thing was bullshit," he said.

"What does that mean?"

"Let's go lie."

"Forever?"

"Forever."

"We take a vow to remain silent about what we did now and forevermore?"

"Done."

At Hancock's office door a few seconds later Charlie stuck out his right hand at Bruce. "My name is Charlie Henderson, by the way."

"Mine is Bruce. Bruce Conn Clark."

"Con?"

"With two *n*'s. It was my mother's maiden name."

"It's been nice doing business with you, Bruce."

"Same here, Charlie."

PART
FOUR

Charlie and Bruce

October 14–24, 1990

Charlie flew USAir to Charlotte, North Carolina, changed planes and then went on to Charleston, South Carolina. Flying had become a source of continuing anger for Charlie. He hated the crowds, the surly attendants, the plastic food, the stupid hub-and-spoke system and most everything else that had happened to America's air transport system since the do-gooders came in and deregulated the airline industry. As he said to Mary Jane and the few others who would listen, it was one of the few times the liberals and conservatives agreed on anything, and that alone should have sent off Screw Alert whistles and bells throughout the land.

The best thing about the trip was the Charleston airport. It was new and fresh and almost empty. Charlie took his time doing the paperwork for the car at the Avis counter. He took his time making a head call. He stopped at a pay phone on his way to the rental-car parking lot. He let the Hillmont phone ring twice and hung up. In two minutes, he let it ring three times before hanging up.

Exactly seventeen minutes later he called the HandiMart number.

She didn't even say hello. She said: "A man named Eller called. Said it was urgent for you to call him. Do you know somebody named Eller?"

"I do," Charlie told Mary Jane. "He's got some property over at Martinsburg he wants to show me."

"Don't lie to me, Charles Henderson."

"Anything else?" he said.

"How about telling me where you are and when you are coming home?"

"I am in a place that is old and hot and I do not know when I will be home."

"Charlie, let me say one thing to you and you listen good to me." Charlie could feel the sting eight hundred miles away. "If you fool around now at your age and get yourself killed I will never forgive you. I will not bury you, I will not even go to your funeral. I will turn your remains over to Jefferson County and let them do with them whatever they wish. And that includes feeding them to the hogs if they'll have you, which they probably won't."

"Got to run," Charlie said. "I love you."

"Sometimes I wonder," she said.

"It's a little late for that."

Several seconds later he was on the phone to Josh Bennett, whose code name in the Berlin operation was "Eller."

"Bad news, Charlie," he said. "Your friend had lunch today with Clay Reynolds, the former CI man. Reynolds said he asked if he had heard from you and he answered no but he was sure Clark didn't believe him. I don't know what that means but I thought you would like to know."

"I do, believe me. Thanks."

"Where are you calling from?"

"From a place old and hot."

Charlie picked up his bag and double-timed out the terminal door to a four-door dark-red Oldsmobile mid-size.

———

Cushing arranged for a car with a driver to meet Bruce at the Charleston airport. That was the normal procedure for Bruce's trips to Kiawah. If Bruce needed something to drive, and he seldom did, Duane had a Jeep and a regular car he could use. Besides, Bruce had gotten out of the habit of driving a car and found that he no longer enjoyed it on those few occasions when he did.

Private planes had a separate hangar and small terminal on the west side of the Charleston airport. The car, a black Lincoln Town Car, drove right up to the door of the plane. The driver, a black man in his forties who Bruce vaguely remembered from a previous trip, took Bruce's small suitcase and put it in the trunk.

Bruce thanked the pilot and the co-pilot from the charter service, climbed in the backseat of the car. It was moving slowly toward the main airport exit at four-thirty P.M., just over an hour after Charlie in his rented Oldsmobile had moved toward the same exit at a much higher rate of speed.

———

There was heavy traffic on Interstate 26, the main highway that ran just north of the airport into Charleston, and parts of it were under construction, which made it all even worse. Charlie got caught in it right at the entrance ramp and was forced to edge along bumper-to-bumper, stop and start, for several minutes before turning off onto Highway 7, a cutoff boulevard that went south across the northwest corner of Charleston to Highway 17.

He made one stop, at a huge Sears store in a shopping center on the way to 17. He bought an air gun, a pistol that looked like a real forty-five automatic and two large boxes of the tiny BBs it fired. He also bought a hunting knife, the kind Boy Scouts take on weekend campouts, and a pair of cheap white sneakers.

He was on U.S. 17 for only a couple of miles before he came to the left turnoff to Kiawah, Seabrook and the other so-called Emerald Islands of South Carolina. Charlie had been to Kiawah once many years ago on a spring vacation with Mary Jane and their children. He thought about those two daughters. They would, each in their own way, go nuts if they knew what he was up to. They almost did when he finally told them what he had been doing for a living all of their lives. The family cover was that he was involved in security work for a big multinational company called Centex which made the cement mixers that went on the back of cement trucks. He told them the truth the weekend after he retired in a session at Hillmont that lasted way, way into Sunday morning. Julie, the youngest, who was then eighteen, and Angela, who was twenty-five, took it hard. They asked if he had ever personally overthrown any governments or helped get arms to right-wing death squads in Central America and other parts of the world. The real trauma came over assassinations. He had to deny he had ever killed or tried to kill the ruler of any foreign country, including most particularly Cuba.

It was the screaming back and forth with Angela about the Kennedy assassination, of all things, that was the most appalling to Charlie.

"Where were you on November 22, 1963, Daddy?" she asked at the top of her lungs.

"In Washington recovering from a goddamn bullet wound!" he hollered back.

"Is that right, Mom?" Angela said to Mary Jane.

"That's right, dear," Mary Jane said.

"What are you saying, goddamn it?" Charlie yelled. "That you do not believe me?"

"I'm saying I don't know what I'm saying."

"I did not kill Kennedy, for Christ's sake!"

"But maybe the CIA did!"

"No!"

"How do you know?"

"I know! Goddamn it, I know!"

There was a lot more screaming and crying before the evening ended, and the strain in the relationships went on for months afterward. Angela remained angry at Charlie and the CIA about everything it had done, real or imagined, but not Julie. She didn't like it that her father had lied to them all this time, but she rather liked the idea of his work and went on to join the Foreign Service. She was now a political-affairs counselor at the embassy in Amman, Jordan, a place Charlie thought was a little too hot for his daughter, but there was nothing he could do—or even say—about that. Charlie felt the same way about the Middle East as he did about airline travel. It was all crazy, a place the U.S. of A. ought to leave to the Middle Easterners to murder and pillage each other about.

He vaguely remembered the turnoff because right after it was a ratty "Members Only—Adults Only" bar called The Dog House. It was nothing more than a two-room shed, but painted on the outside were a man and woman dancing—more or less life-sized. From there the narrow two-lane road went by a large tomato-processing facility, more beer joints, rundown service stations, a few churches, some shacks and many tiny houses until finally, after fifteen miles or so, the road became overhung by tall trees and moss. And then, suddenly, was the sign to Kiawah. Charlie noticed and remembered how pretty it got before the turn, but mostly he got impatient over how long it was taking.

The entrance road into Kiawah was like that to a large country club or planned upper-class housing development. The palm trees were perfectly placed along both sides of the road, which was a well-cared-for blacktop that led first to a Visitors Registration Office and a security gate and guardhouse not unlike that at CIA headquarters and similarly secure places.

Charlie signed up for a room at the Kiawah Inn and went through the gate a few minutes later with a guest card on the dashboard of his car.

The Lincoln Town Car with Bruce in its backseat came through the same gate one hour and twenty minutes later.

Bruce had spent almost no time looking out the window. He had made this trip down that Low Country road many times before, so there was nothing more for him to see. He read *An American Life,* Ronald Reagan's memoirs that had just been published. He began reading it like any other book, one word at a time, but after a while he was reading only every other paragraph or so, and then he was only glancing at the words to see if anything jumped off the page at him. It was seldom that anything did. Bruce found the book as eerily disconnected to reality as the man had been to his presidency.

Kiawah was an island resort originally developed in what was called "Barbados plantation style" by the Kuwaitis, the very people who were at the center of Saddam Hussein's and the world's attention at the moment. The Kuwaitis sold it after a few years and it was now owned and operated by a consortium of American investors, including some South Carolinians. The island was three miles wide and ten long, with eight miles of the whitest, widest, hardest beaches on the East Coast. Bruce had been to all the big ones, including those on the Cape and on Long Island, Martha's Vineyard and Nantucket, and he thought no others were even in the same league as Kiawah's. Along the beach and back inland on a bay were three golf courses designed by famous golfers like Jack Nicklaus, two tennis clubs with scores of courts and a variety of condominiums and private homes. The Inn, where Charlie was staying, was in the center of the most built-up area, which had two bars, three restaurants and several small gift and clothing stores.

Bruce's car kept going past the turnoff into the Inn, continuing on the main road another two miles to the main residential area. There was another guard station to pass through before winding down a subsidiary blacktop road through pine and palm trees to his brother's house.

Duane had not been told he was coming, but that kind of thing no longer mattered.

There was some difference in price, but Charlie took a room on the beach side. Might as well get something out of this before I die, he thought. It was really only an excuse for wasting some money. He had no intention of dying right now or any other time soon. That was the reason why he still exercised and watched what he ate and why he had decided to mount a defense against Bruce Conn Clark, a defense based on the football and Agency-warrior maxim that the best defense was a good offense.

The first thing he did when he got inside the room was to find Duane Clark's name in the local phone book. The address was 6718 Pine Needle Circle. He wrote that down on a sheet of paper from a Kiawah Inn memo pad and then found it on the map of the island that came with his check-in packet. Then he changed into a green short-sleeved pullover shirt he had bought weeks ago at Martinsburg, a pair of khaki trousers and the new Sears sneakers.

It was already after five o'clock. He had to keep moving.

He went to the bicycle-rental shed just across the entrance circle of the Inn, showed them his guest charge card and rode away on a big-tire bike. Instead of heading down the road, he went the other way, toward the beach. He found a wooden-plank path that went over the sand dune and down to the beach.

Charlie had forgotten how wonderful that beach was. Hard as concrete, almost as white as snow, more beautiful than any he had seen anywhere else in the world.

He rode west, with the water to his right. There were only a few people out walking or riding bikes, but it would not have mattered. The beach was forty yards wide, so it was impossible to be there and not believe it was all yours. That was also true of those waves. Mary Jane, who was the one in the family who always pushed to go to a beach on vacation, believed God's most wondrous creation after a healthy newly born baby was an ocean wave. She often said her only regret in life was that she had not been a poet so she could write poems only about waves, only about the hypnotic rhythms and hammering sounds of those magic creations that were always there to remind humans of their own smallness, their own insignificance.

Charlie stopped every few minutes for bearings, matching what he saw on his map with the condos and the houses and other things he saw on his left.

Finally, way down the beach where the condos ended and the big houses began, he came to what he decided was the match he wanted: 6718 Pine Needle Circle. There were some wooden steps that led to a walkway across the dune to the house. It was a large two-story frame structure covered in pale blue shingles that resembled something you would see on Nantucket, Mary Jane's girlhood place where she and Charlie and their family had also gone on several vacations.

Was it the house where Duane Clark lived? There was no way to tell for sure from this far away, which was about thirty yards. So? So it was time to take a risk. Was Bruce already there? Unlikely. Simple matter of time. Had he called his brother ahead of time to warn him? Maybe.

Charlie leaned down and with a harsh movement scraped the inside of his left forearm against one of the bike pedals. It drew a little blood. He did it again. More blood came.

He took a handkerchief out of his right hip pocket, slapped it against the wound and started running up the steps past a small sign that said PRIVATE PROPERTY—NO EXIT, NO TRESPASSING.

"Hello!" he yelled. "Is there anyone home? Hello!"

He saw a male figure appear at a sliding-glass door on the second floor. Charlie kept walking fast toward the house, holding his arm out in front of him.

By the time Charlie got to the house, to a door on the first floor, it was open and a man was standing there. He was in his late sixties, dressed in white duck pants, a bright yellow short-sleeved shirt and open-toe leather sandals with no socks. His hair was gray and long, well cut and well combed.

"I fell off my bike," Charlie said to him. "Could I wash off and maybe borrow a Band-Aid or something?"

The man frowned with concern and said, "Certainly. Come right here into the kitchen."

Charlie followed him inside to a kitchen that was modern and huge. Is this Duane Clark? He looks nothing like Bruce, thought Charlie. Of course, they could have had different fathers or something. He's also younger than he should be. Duane Clark should be in his late seventies at least.

The man, whoever he was, went to the kitchen sink, turned on the cold water, handed Charlie a soft dishtowel and stood aside. Charlie, Mr. Grateful himself, gushed with gratitude, stepped forward and washed off his wound. He hoped the man did not notice how truly insignificant a cut it was. There was a window there at the sink and Charlie could see out to a garage that contained two vehicles—an old Mercedes and a Jeep—and the driveway. There was a number over the rural-style mailbox. It said 6718, the number in the phone book for Duane Clark.

"Boy, I really do appreciate this," Charlie said. "Good samaritans are hard to find on the roads of life anymore."

"I am just so glad I could help," said the man as Charlie turned around, dried off his arm.

"Wasn't much to it after all," Charlie said apologetically. "Again, thank you. Do you happen to have a Band-Aid?"

"We do indeed," said the man. "They are upstairs. I will run and get one."

"I'll go with you," said Charlie, moving right with the man

through the doorway to the rest of the house. "Somebody at the Inn told me Sam Shepard and Jessica Lange, you know, the movie stars, had a house down on this part of the island. Is that right?"

"No, no," said the man, leading the way up a flight of stairs. "No celebrities here."

"He said something else about a big-time Washington guy, too. A former secretary of defense or state or something like that."

The man laughed. "He was referring probably to Secretary Bruce Conn Clark. He doesn't live here but his brother does."

"Yeah, yeah," said Charlie, ever so casually and dumbly. "That was it."

"This is Mr. Duane Clark's house you're in, as a matter of fact," said the man with pride.

"Well, what do you know?" Charlie said. They were on the second floor now. Charlie noticed an open door to a bedroom on the beach side. A man was lying under covers in the center of a four-poster bed. His eyes were open but they were looking upward at the ceiling. There was no doubt he was Duane Clark. Even with a quick side-view look, it was obvious that he was an older, grayer version of Bruce Conn Clark.

The other man had kept going to a bathroom down the hall, so Charlie, after only a slight pause, had to move on, too.

"Is that Mr. Clark there in that bedroom?" he said when he got to the bathroom.

"That's the dear man himself, yes, indeed," said the man, handing Charlie a Band-Aid.

Charlie put the Band-Aid on and then moved back down the hall behind the man. "I guess it would be too much to ask to meet him?" Charlie asked.

"He doesn't meet well anymore."

Charlie got another quick glance at Duane Clark as they went by the bedroom door again. Bruce's brother had not moved. He was still lying straight with his eyes open. Charlie took note also that there was a sliding-glass door to the outside from the room.

Back in the kitchen, he again said thank you and left, making a quick, silent stop at the Mercedes before heading toward the beach.

———————

Charlie had been gone less than fifteen minutes when Bruce's car drove up in the driveway. The man in the white pants was out the door and to the car before Bruce could get out with his small suitcase.

"Bruce!" said the man. "Say, 'Surprise!' "

"Surprise, Ancel," said Bruce. They shook hands vigorously. The man insisted on taking Bruce's suitcase from him and they walked together into the house.

"Why didn't you call or something?" said Ancel. "My goodness, one little call and I would have had something special ready for dinner. As it is I have not a thing ready, not a thing really good enough for you."

"I was on my way from Miami back to Washington and just decided to stop in," Bruce said. "It was spur of the moment."

Bruce and the man he called Ancel went into the kitchen. Bruce wanted a drink of water. He immediately spotted the dishtowel with traces of blood on it. "What happened here?" he asked.

"A man on the beach had an accident on his bicycle," said Ancel. "He ran up here in search of medical care and comfort and he, of course, found it."

"Was it serious?"

"Oh, no. Just a scratch."

Bruce took a long gulp of water, thought for a full minute and then asked: "What did the man look like?"

"Why, my goodness, what difference does it make what he looked like?"

"Oh, just curious."

Ancel laughed and then went on to describe Charlie Henderson. "Did he ask about Duane?"

"Oh, no, he thought Sam Shepard and Jessica Lange lived around here," Ancel said. "I don't know how it came up but I finally told him only your brother did."

Oh, Charlie, thought Bruce. You are good, you really are.

"Did he see Duane?" Bruce asked Ancel.

"Oh, just a peak as we went by the door, maybe."

———————

Charlie stopped on the way back down the beach. He picked up a couple of beautifully fanned crab shells. He fingered them, admired them and thought of Mary Jane. Assuming everything worked out all right, he would never tell her he had come to Kiawah and its magnificent beach. It would really piss her off to know he had come without her no matter why he had come.

Off in the water not more than a mile away, a shrimp boat was coming by. Then came another. And another. The noise of the waves drowned out the sound of their motors. What kind of life must that be? Get up early in the morning, ride a boat out to sea, throw out nets all day, fill the bottom of your boat with fish and then motor back in. Day after day the same thing. For the thirty years he was with the Agency he never really did the same thing two days in a row. Now at Hillmont, he still didn't.

Streaks of orange were now across the darkening horizon. The sun was going down.

Where are you, Mr. Bruce Conn Clark, code name "Mark"? Have you arrived? Did you bring Jay Buckner with you? You're a chickenshit if you did!

Buckner or not, Charlie had already concluded he needed a helper of his own.

Back at the Inn, he secured his bike with a lock in a rack and walked into the main lobby, where there was a sitting room in addition to a front desk. Across an enclosed porch were the restaurants, a fancy one called Charleston Gallery and a more modest one called Jasmine Porch. A separate bar was upstairs. Charlie walked around casually as if he were a newly arrived guest checking out the premises. He was really checking out people—bell captains, desk clerks, hostesses and waiters—for a likely recruit. It had been a while since he had done "asset spotting," as it was called in the Agency, and it made him feel good to be doing it again. In his prime, he was a master. Show him the files and faces of twelve Russian second naval attachés and he could spot with remarkable accuracy the one who was vulnerable to an approach.

Now, the question was, which one of these employees of the Kiawah Inn could do what I need done, and which one of those would be the most recruitable?

He finally zeroed in on the bell captain, a tall black man dressed in a short-sleeved green, brown and white uniform that resembled that of a Third World national army officer.

Charlie, still the curious let-me-soak-it-all-in arrivee, went out to the bell stand and just stood for a few seconds. The bell captain was there by himself. All was quiet. They exchanged pleasant smiles. The captain nodded.

"Wonderful evening, sir," said the captain finally.

"My God, is it like this all of the time?" Charlie asked.

"Every day except when it rains or hurricanes," said the captain.

Charlie, Mr. Charm, laughed.

"First time here?" asked the captain.

"Right. But it won't be the last. Depending on what happens to my friend."

"Oh?"

"Yeah, he's dying. Lives in a house down the island. Name is Clark. Do you know him?"

"Clark? No, sir. Don't believe I do. No, sir."

"I've come to surprise him. He doesn't know I'm here. I'm going to do some good-natured kidding around with him before I tell him."

"Oh, that'll be fun. Yes, sir."

Charlie sighed as if in sadness, and took a step back toward the lobby inside. "You don't know of anybody I could hire to help me, do you, Captain? Somebody to help me line up some folks to make some phone calls, maybe run some peculiar errands?"

"Well, I sure do, sir, and you are looking right at him."

The captain said his name was Owens. Raymond Owens. Charlie said he was Donald Coppell, the name he had used to register at the Inn. A false identity was one of the tools of his warrior trade that he had not given up. He had kept Donald Coppell alive after leaving the Agency with a Visa card, a D.C. driver's license and other things. Why? Insurance. Insurance for what? Maybe it was just out of habit. Maybe one of the retirement consultancies would require such a thing. Maybe this, maybe that.

⸻

The phone rang at 6718 Pine Needle Circle an hour later. Ancel got it on the third ring.

"This is the message center at the Inn," said a deep male voice.

"Yes, um?" said Ancel.

"We have an envelope here for Mr. Bruce Conn Clark that Federal Express delivered," said the man. "It's from some faraway place like Washington, D.C. Are you Mr. Clark?"

"No, dear, I am not, but he is here and I will tell him," Ancel said. "Somebody will be down to get it real soon."

"Thank you."

Ancel told Bruce about the call. His immediate thought was that Cushing had sent him something he had forgotten to put in his briefcase. Probably a further report on the Japanese textile matter. It could wait till morning. On the other hand, why not take a drive down to the Inn? He might even run into Charlie Henderson, code name "George."

Ancel said he would be glad to make the trip, but Bruce insisted.

A few minutes later he backed his brother's ten-year-old light

tan Mercedes sedan out of the garage and headed down the winding road toward the Inn.

There was a stop sign where Pine Needle intersected with the
main Island Road. He stopped and then turned the steering wheel
hard to the left and gunned the car.

Instead of turning, the car shot straight ahead. He slammed on
the brakes. The car skidded gently into a sturdy grove of tall pine
trees on the other side of the road. Bruce, who had not put on his
seat belt, was thrown forward against the steering wheel. It
knocked out his wind but he was not otherwise hurt.

What's next, Charlie? A bomb in my room?

A Kiawah policeman was at the scene in a few minutes, having
simply come upon the accident while making a regular patrol
round. Bruce assured him that he did not need medical treatment
of any kind. A wrecker was summoned to haul off the Mercedes to
a garage that the cop said "did good work" on foreign cars. It was
ten miles down the main road toward Charleston. Bruce told the
wrecker driver to ask the mechanic to check the steering column
for a clean cut. And while he was at it he might also give all the
hoses a good inspection.

The policeman drove Bruce back to Duane's house. The first
thing Bruce did was to go right to the kitchen and call the Kiawah
Inn message desk. A young female voice answered.

"This is Bruce Conn Clark." He gave his address and phone
number and said: "It seems I will not be able to pick up that
envelope tonight after all. I'll be around in the morning."

"Do you want me to send it down with a bellman?" said the
young voice.

"That would be fine. Thank you." He gave her the address on
Pine Needle.

Bruce hung up, somewhat surprised that there was a real package for him. But before he could take more than two or three steps, the phone rang. He picked it up. It was the young female voice at the message center. "Mr. Clark, I have checked everything and we don't have any package for you."

"Well, I must have misunderstood. Thank you."

That's better, Charlie. You bastard.

―――――――

Charlie found a spot on the beach side of the dune with an unobstructed view of the top floors of the house. He stretched out fully on his stomach and rested the air pistol on a piece of driftwood he had brought along from the beach. It was a clear night, the moon was at slightly more than three quarters. It was just after midnight. The house, some twenty yards away, was dark.

He sighted in on a sliding-glass door and pulled the trigger. There was only a slight *pop!* when it fired. Then a slight *click!* as the BB hit glass. He fired at a window. A light came on. He fired again at the window. And again and again. Another light in another room came on.

He stopped firing. In a minute or so the sliding-glass door was opened. It was Bruce. He had on a robe and pajamas, both of which shone from the light behind him.

"Yes, Charlie, what is it?" yelled out Bruce toward the beach.

Charlie smiled. But he did not answer.

"Okay," Bruce yelled. "You got me up. What now?"

Charlie took another sighting. And waited.

Bruce said nothing else. After another minute he turned to go back inside.

Charlie pulled the trigger again. *Pop!*

"Damn!" Bruce yelled and slapped his left buttock with his left hand. He turned back around to the beach. "Charlie, you bastard! You made your point!"

Bruce stepped back inside the room and slammed the door closed. Ancel, also in pajamas and robe, was crouched down behind a red overstuffed chair.

"What point?" Ancel said. "What point? Who is Charlie? Bruce, my goodness, what is happening?"

Bruce's eye went to a tiny little copper BB on the floor at his feet. He leaned over and picked it up. "This is the point." He held out the BB to Ancel.

"A BB?" said Ancel. "Somebody is shooting BBs at us? Why in the world would somebody do that? That's what little boys do."

"Whatever, it's over," Bruce said. "Why don't you go back to bed now."

"What about you?"

"I may throw on some clothes and run an errand," Bruce said. He could barely conceal his excitement. Here I come, Charlie!

They both left the room after turning out the light and never doing more than glancing at the man who was fast asleep in a large four-poster bed in the center of the room.

———————————

Several minutes later Charlie, still lying against the dune, heard a door close. Then, after a few seconds, the whirring sound of a car starter. It must be the Jeep, Charlie thought. Who in the hell would be going out at this hour? Bruce? The brother? That other guy? All three of them? Where would he or they be going?

He listened to the Jeep being backed up and driven away. He pulled himself up. He did so just in time to see the headlights through the pine trees as the Jeep sped away down the road.

Charlie crept back down the dune and, in a low crouch, returned to the beach and to his rented bike.

It was a magnificent evening. He decided to take his time getting back to the Inn. He stopped three or four times, dismounted the bike, tossed rocks and shells into the surf. Once he just sat down on the sand and watched the moon reflect off the water.

It was late but he was not tired. As he put his room key into the lock he wasn't even sure he could go to sleep. His brain and his heart and his spirit were racing.

He took a step inside and reached for the light switch. He felt something against his right foot. A trip cord, he thought, as he went sprawling flat on his face.

With his face still into the rug, the first thing he did was determine that he was not hurt. No bones broken, nothing. He pulled himself to his feet and closed the door.

The trip cord was a piece of thin rope tied across the bottom of the door. One end was fixed to a leg of a small writing table, the other to the leg of a dresser.

Then he noticed a piece of Kiawah Inn memo-pad paper on the little table. In big handwritten block letters was written: WHAT IF THERE HAD BEEN A BOMB ATTACHED TO THE ROPE? SLEEP TIGHT, CHARLIE.

Charlie awoke to the phone ringing on the night table to his left. He counted to three, remembered where he was and picked up the receiver.

"Clark here," said Bruce.

"Henderson here," said Charlie.

"I propose a temporary pause in our conflict for talk."

"Why?"

"Because we are mature adults."

"I'm not so sure of that."

Bruce, talking on the phone in his brother's kitchen, agreed with Charlie. But he said, "I'll meet you on the beach in twenty minutes."

"Where on the beach?"

"Halfway between the Inn and here. Don't bring that stupid BB gun."

"Don't bring Buckner."

"He's not here. What did you think of my rope trick?"

"See you in twenty minutes."

———————

They nodded and Charlie even grinned, but they did not shake hands or otherwise demonstrate anything but cool calm to each other. Bruce pointed back toward the direction he had come as if to ask if that way to walk was all right with Charlie.

"Sure," Charlie said. He looked around in all four directions and added, "You sure you haven't got some tech-services hood out there taking a bead on me?"

"The white flag of truce is up, Charlie. Did you leave your pop gun at home?"

Charlie patted the pockets of his khakis and held his arms up over his head. "Clean, sir."

"If that was a real weapon you were firing you would have killed me last night," Bruce said.

"That was exactly the point I wanted to make, sir."

"Cut out the 'sir' shit if you don't mind. That was the same point I wanted to make with my little rope trick."

"You made it. It never occurred to me you would actually get your own hands dirty doing anything. And I assumed for some reason—hoped, I guess—that you had left Buckner at home."

They were walking now. It was still early, just after seven-thirty. The sun was out but few other people besides Charlie and Bruce were. They had the freshly washed white sand pretty much to themselves.

"Are you going to make me go through it all question by question," said Charlie, "or will you just tell me what in the hell this is all about?"

Bruce leaned down and picked up a shell. It was the size of a silver dollar, coarse gray on one side, porcelain white on the other. He ran his fingers across the smooth side to remove the sand and then threw it side-armed toward the water. It skipped once and then disappeared into the surf.

Bruce decided this was his last chance. Either he told his story and told it well now or somebody had to die, and he was going to do everything he could to make sure it was Charlie Henderson. Charlie had nothing to lose but his life. Bruce had everything to lose.

The rope thing had really upset Charlie. He didn't realize how much until he tried to go to sleep. He couldn't. So he turned on the TV, but nothing was on except CNN and the news no longer entertained him. He tried to read *Chinaman's Chance,* a Ross Thomas paperback he had brought along, but he couldn't concentrate. It wouldn't take. So mostly he laid there in the bed wide awake until a couple of hours before Bruce's call. Something was going to have to give. It was fun, but on the other hand it was stupid. Kill or be killed? Two old farts playing little-boy spy games. Come on! Mary Jane, I love you.

Bruce hadn't slept well either. But what kept him awake was simple little-boy exhilaration. First from using smiles and twenty-dollar bills with a bellman and a room clerk at the Inn to get a fix on Charlie, the name he was checked in under and his room number. Then from slipping a tiny wire into the door lock and opening it. It had been twenty-five years since he had broken into anything like that, years since he had done anything that made him feel so young and good about himself.

Bruce took the long, deep breath of a sixty-seven-year-old man and said: "I doubt if you remember that I got a call from my brother that evening of the Kennedy assassination. It was while we were in our little closed room, the one you wanted to smell up with your cigar smoke."

"I only smoked it outside. Now you can't smoke anything anywhere . . ."

"They said it was urgent. Well, it was. Duane, using a sloppy form of cryptic language, told me a Russian agent had just left his office in Poughkeepsie. The agent wanted him to call me and tell me they didn't have anything to do with shooting Kennedy."

Charlie stopped walking. "I don't get it."

"Cambridge. It was because of Cambridge. My brother was only there for a year in the early thirties before my father made him come home. But he was there long enough to find sex as well as art history as well as pseudo—left-wing politics in common with Anthony Blunt and the boys."

"Anthony and the boys weren't pseudo-anything."

"Duane was in his political beliefs."

They were moving again.

"The night before Duane left Cambridge, Blunt took him out to a night of food, drink and fun and tried to recruit him as an 'agent of the Comintern,' as it was called. He wouldn't be asked to do anything now but maybe down the line, particularly if Duane went into some form of government service. Blunt gave Duane one half of a card, a queen of hearts—the pun was intended—and said if anyone ever showed up with the other half he should do whatever he could to help. Duane was drunk and stupid enough to take the half of the card and keep it."

"When did he tell you about it?"

"It was a long time later. A long, critical time later. There is a ten-year difference in age between Duane and me. I was an accident, a lucky one for America and the world, as my father said, but an accident nevertheless. Duane saw me much the way an uncle would see a nephew, rather than as a brother he could talk to about important things like what happened to him with Blunt. He might have never mentioned it, in fact, if I hadn't told him through veiled and sloppy talk that I was going with 'the government' to do something I could not talk about. He took me to dinner at the Plaza in New York and told me about Blunt and the card. Nothing had happened since, nobody had shown up with the other half. He had gone on to become a nonpolitical professor of art history and he assumed it was all over. But he did want me to know. I said I appreciated his telling me but I really didn't. It was the kind of thing I wished I did not know. I was worried from then on that I would get caught by a flutter or something or someday some guy in a dark suit with an accent would show up with the half a card. And eventually he did. On November 22, 1963."

"So you're telling me you manipulated our big decision that day."

"No, no. At least I hope not."

"Hope? Come on. You did it for the Russians or you didn't."

"Back off, Charlie. I can't remember what was really going on in my mind then. I remember believing the Russians killed Kennedy and I remember believing we'd be fools to say so to McCone. That would have been true in any case. And it doesn't matter now anyhow."

"Doesn't matter my ass!"

"I mean, goddamn it, that we stand here twenty-seven years later with the certain knowledge that the Russians had nothing to do with it. Have you paid any attention to all that has come out about the assassination since that night?"

"Certainly."

"Well, then you know there is not one shred of evidence the Russians were involved with it. There is not one assassination expert, no matter how kooky, who believes they were. So we were right to do what we did . . ."

"For the wrong reasons."

"Can you think of a better reason than trying to prevent a nuclear war?"

They were almost to the end of the island now. There were no more houses back off across the dunes on the left. Straight ahead there was water and far ahead across it was the land that led eventually to Charleston.

"So you figured from what I said at DeCarlo's that night that I might tell the world about our McCone assignment?" Charlie said.

"Oh, yes. Oh, yes."

"For somebody who is supposed to be so smart you are really so stupid. Something out in the public now about what we did in 1963 would not have been a problem for you."

"Think about it, Charlie. If you tell our story, the Russian connection through Duane follows like a rainbow after a rain."

"I don't follow."

"*Glasnost* and all of that. KGB files and defectors are going to be everywhere. Somewhere sometime some enterprising type is going to discover a case report from some Soviet agent who paid a visit to the brother of later-to-be Secretary of State Bruce Conn Clark. The agent, I am sure, probably takes full credit for the fact that the Soviets did not get blamed for the assassination, particularly during those first few hours and days. For the guy who finds the report, his day, his career and his bank account will be made."

They turned around and started back the other way.

"How in the hell did they know your brother had a brother in the Agency?" Charlie asked. "Weren't you full covert?"

"I was."

"How did they know?"

"I have no idea and I don't want to guess."

"I'll give you two even bigger how-in-the-hells. How in the hell did the Russians know you were in Washington, and how in the hell did they know you were working on the assassination investigation?"

"They might have assumed everyone in the Agency was."

"Sure. And Jesus is alive and well living across the water there in Charleston with Elvis."

"What are you getting at?" Bruce asked.

"Only that that other Jesus—James Jesus Angleton—may not have been so crazy after all with his hunts for moles behind every Agency door."

They walked in silence for a good three minutes.

"Did they ever come back?" Charlie asked finally.

"Who?"

"The Russians, did they hit your brother again?"

"Oh, no. It was a one-shotter."

"He was lucky. They usually come back."

"I wouldn't call Duane 'lucky,' " Bruce said. "You saw him, I understand?"

"Barely."

"Three years ago he was walking this very beach and suddenly was hit by a headache, a terrible headache. He sat down and then he lay down. And that was the last time he moved. The headache was a stroke, which resulted in something the experts call Locked-In Syndrome. He has all of his faculties but he cannot move anything except his eyelids. He just lies there day after day and he will continue to do so until the day he dies."

"I'm sorry."

Now they were at the steps that led across the dune to 6718 Pine Needle Circle.

"I have to have your answer about where we go from here," Bruce said.

"You win," said Charlie. "I quit. Our secret holds."

"Just like that. 'You win. I quit.' "

"Just like that."

"Why? Why so easy?"

"I'm tired, Mr. Clark. I'm over my head. I do not need this. I do not want to continue this old-warriors duel with you. I will lose. You have too many horses and Indians. When my time comes to go I will go quietly, anonymously, just like Jack Douglas. Our little game is over."

"It's over?"

"My kids and grandkids will just have to live without knowing how I saved the world from a nuclear holocaust. I'm sure you realize that I am only one of your problems. Those KGB files may turn you and your brother up anyhow sometime . . ."

"Thank you, Charlie," Bruce said. He stuck out his right hand. Charlie did not take it.

"You would have had me killed if I had come down the other way, wouldn't you?" Charlie said.

"I would have had no choice. I have invested too much in my life to have lost it all at the very end."

And they walked away from each other.

—————

Bruce left the Charleston airport several hours after Charlie. The private jet flew nonstop to National Airport, where a car and driver picked him up and took him to the Watergate. There was nobody at the apartment, but of course there never was at night. He was usually delighted that it was empty of other people, other voices, other needs, other humans' things. But tonight he wanted something else besides just himself. It was the first time he had felt that way in a very long time. Maybe ever. It was a thought that made him laugh out loud.

Bruce Conn Clark was a man of organized habit and neatness. He always did the same things when he came in from a trip. Go first to the bedroom, unpack the suitcase, change into comfortable clothes, look at the mail and the phone messages and, depending on the time of day, have a glass of Perrier or grapefruit juice.

This time, he set his small suitcase down in the entrance hall, removed only his suit coat and threw it on a chair in the living room. He went to the bar with the idea of opening a small bottle of Perrier. The bar was inside a paneled mahogany cabinet that looked like an eighteenth-century Georgian bookcase. He opened a door. His eye skipped over the Perrier to an unopened bottle of Stolichnaya vodka sitting there on the shelf along with an assortment of other liquor and liqueurs. Stolichnaya had been his drink of choice back in the days when there was such a thing in his life. He drank it ice-cold straight-up "neat," he drank it over ice with an olive as a vermouthless martini, he drank it with tomato juice and seasoning as a Bloody Mary and he drank it with orange juice and with tonic water. How long, oh Lord, has it been since a sip of that silvery wonder has been down my throat? he asked himself. Fifteen years?

He took the bottle in both hands, broke the seal with a knife and removed the cap. He poured two inches into a whiskey tumbler and then added two ice cubes from the ice machine in the small refrigerator built into the bar.

The view from his front-room window was to the west, over the river toward Georgetown. What he mostly could see was the new waterfront complex called Harbor Town, which was a lit-up conglomeration of four-story office buildings, restaurants, apartments and a few shops around a large fountain that spewed water through colored lighting.

He went to the window, held his glass up toward Georgetown and said, "To life, liberty and the pursuit of happiness." He took a long gulp of the vodka. The ice had made it cold, but not as cold as it would have been had it been kept in the freezer as he used to do. It burned a bit as it went down his throat. Like those old and happy times.

"To the president of the United States," he said. And took another healthy swallow.

"To Queen Elizabeth the Second," he said, taking another.

"To the prime minister of Upper Volta," he said, taking one more. Upper Volta was among his least favorite nations of the world.

"To the Danish deputy underminister for interplanetary affairs," he said, finishing the glass. Denmark was among his most favorite nations of the world.

He returned to the bar, placed two more ice cubes in the glass and poured in two more inches of vodka.

Cushing had left a blue folder of items on the small desk by a window that opened out to the southwest, across the water to Arlington National Cemetery. Bruce went over, sat down, drank some more vodka and opened the folder.

There were Cushing memos about invitations to talk about what-to-do-about-Saddam-Hussein from seven television programs including *Good Morning America, MacNeil/Lehrer* and *Meet the Press.* There were five social invitations, all to events in the next two days, all to events that sounded awful. He took each one and tore it into little pieces and dropped them on the floor. There was a letter from the president of Princeton University asking him to serve on some kind of advisory committee that would hold international seminars on the New World Order in international affairs. He tore it into five pieces and threw it on the floor. He did the same, between sips of vodka, to two honorary-degree-in-exchange-for-commencement-address offers, to three reference requests and to one inquiry from an author writing a book about United States–China relations in the 1990s.

He was hungry. He grabbed the telephone receiver on the desk and dialed 411. "Information, what city?" said a female.

"Washington, D.C., the capital of the free world," said Bruce. "I want someplace that will bring me something to eat."

"Do you have a name and an address."

"Yes, indeed, I do. Bruce Conn Clark, the Watergate."

"No, sir. I meant the food place."

"No."

"What kind of food, sir?"

"You name it."

"Pizza?"

"Young lady, I have not had a piece of pizza in my mouth in fifteen years. No, young lady, make that seventeen years. Not in seventeen years."

"Sir, this is the telephone-information operator."

"Pizza, yes, a pizza. I'll have a pizza with everything except anchovies. Send it right over. I detest anchovies."

"Sir, I can give you a number but that is all."

"Good-bye," he said and hung up.

It took some doing, but he got to his feet and lurched back to the window that had the view toward Georgetown.

"Charlie Henderson," he said, holding his glass up, "I thank you. I commend you. I implore you. Please leave it alone. I beg of you.

I beg of you, Charlie Henderson. I thank you. I praise you. I beg of you. I beg of you, Charlie Henderson. Please, Charlie Henderson. Please, Charlie Henderson. Do not destroy me, Charlie Henderson. I am at your mercy, Charlie Henderson. Stick with your decision, Charlie Henderson. Please, please, please. Do not think, Charlie Henderson. Listen to me, listen to me, Charlie Henderson. Charlie Henderson! Charlie Henderson!"

The glass slipped out of his hand and fell to the floor, but the heavy beige carpet caught it. It did not break, there was no noise.

He took four lunging steps toward a leather couch across the room. Halfway, he stopped and sunk slowly to his knees, lay down on the carpet and passed out. It was the first time he had done such a thing in fifteen years.

Make that seventeen.

———

Charlie slept that night in his own bed at Hillmont. He had taken the subway from National Airport to Union Station and then the train back to Duffields, where Mary Jane met him. And scolded him.

"Never again, Charlie," she said the second the doors were closed on the Wagoneer and they were moving. "Never, ever. I will not go through this. I will not. I am not kidding. I am more serious about this than anything we have ever had between us. I mean anything. Stop it. Stop it right now. Whatever it is, stop it. I will not have it. You stop it or I will. I am deadly serious."

Charlie's choice of weapon in such exchanges of fire with Mary Jane had always been silence. Let her talk and rave and scream and whatever, nod and smile with understanding and concern, but say nothing in return. It did not work this time.

"Say something, Charlie," she said. "Say something that makes sense. Say it now or else."

"Or else what?"

"Or I will proceed to make your life absolutely one hundred percent miserable."

"Doing what?"

"Telling the grandchildren you are the Devil, throwing out all of the Calvados, inviting Jane and Red Albers for dinner once a week for a year, destroying your American Express and Master-Charge and Visa cards so you can't buy shirts at Martinsburg. Things like that."

"I can handle everything but the Alberses," Charlie said. Jane and Red Albers were a retired husband-and-wife lawyer team from Baltimore who lived five miles west of Hillmont. Both were redheaded, both liked to talk at the same time, both had nothing to say except things about their seven grandchildren and their Methodist Church and both were 1960s liberals who thought the CIA was an instrument of evil that should be abolished.

As she drove the Wagoneer into the Hillmont road, Mary Jane made one final plea: "Will you at least tell me what you are doing and why?"

Charlie said, "Oh, sweetheart, I really would like to. I really would. But I can't. Not now."

"Is it official business? Tell me that."

"It is but it isn't," he said. "It's some unfinished official business that I am trying to finish unofficially, is probably the best way to put it."

"Are you in danger of some kind?"

"No, no."

"I don't believe you."

"I'm sorry."

"When will it be over?"

"Maybe in a day or two. I hope so, at least. What's cooking with you?"

"None of your business," said Mary Jane. "Except I found two more copies of the book."

"Terrific. Where?"

"At a flea market in Middleway. They're in great shape. I've already put them in the rooms."

The book was *Act of Darkness,* a 1935 novel written by John Peale Bishop. He had grown up around Charles Town, where he had set his novel about a prominent man's rape of his wife's friend. It was based on a real event in the history of Jefferson County, and one of the homes described in detail in the book was Hillmont. That was the particular reason Mary Jane and Charlie wanted a copy in each guest room.

She turned off the motor and moved the gear-shift lever to park. "God, how I wish I didn't love you."

"That's a nice thing to say after forty years."

"You are sixty-four years old, Charlie Henderson. That is too old to be playing spy. Way, way too old."

It was something he did not have to be told.

"The good news, my dear," he said, "is that what I have left to do is right around here."

"Here?"

"In the neighborhood, in the area."

"Well, thank God for the little things."

She had fixed him his favorite dinner, meatloaf with a baked potato. They ate together in the dining room with a half-bottle of a good red Bordeaux and a fire going in the fireplace.

"You really are too old for this kind of thing, Charlie."

"You already said that," he replied. And he already said to himself that he did not have to be told.

But there was something else he had to do. Just one more thing. There was something about Bruce Conn Clark and his story that did not ring true. It rang with the jarring sound of a goddamn lie.

Charlie had been sitting in the waiting area of Gate 22 at the Charlotte airport that morning when it hit him. When he recalled that November 1963 session with James Jesus Angleton. What did he say about the obvious not being so obvious if it is too obvious?

He had still had twenty minutes before his connecting flight to Washington National was leaving. Charlie folded up and tossed away the *Charlotte Observer* he was reading and went to a pay phone. He had many calls to make. Many, many calls.

The fact that he was really too old for this kind of thing had to be ignored for just a few more days.

======

Bruce woke up the first time around three A.M. His head felt like somebody was pounding it with a wooden mallet, his insides were in his throat. He got up off the floor and stumbled into the nearest bathroom, a small powder room seldom used except by dinner and cocktail-party guests. It was sweet-smelling and interior-decorated with flowered wallpaper and towels.

Bruce flipped up the commode seat, went to his knees, stuck his head over the rim and threw up everything he had in him to throw up. It wasn't long before he was only heaving and spitting, and he crawled away out into the hall, curled up and closed his eyes. Water, he wanted water. A drink of ice-cold water. With aspirin. Ten aspirin. A thousand aspirin! No, no. It would not stay down. Neither would stay down. None would stay down.

He went to sleep again and stayed out for five more hours, when he was shaken awake by Kermit Cushing.

"Sir, are you all right? Sir, sir. What happened? Sir?"

Cushing helped him to the leather couch he could not reach on his own the night before.

"Don't talk to me, Cushing," Bruce said. His face felt flushed, his mouth had a taste of dead dried animal. His head, his stomach and every other feeling part of his body ached. He looked down at his maroon silk tie. Why didn't I take it off? It was splattered with little spots of what he had tossed into the commode.

Please, Charlie Henderson!

An old friend at the Yorktown Foundation did the final work for Charlie in arranging his rendezvous with Alexander Gannady Petrov, alias "Top Hat." Yorktown was created by the Agency and other like-minded organizations to help Soviet bloc defectors establish new lives in America. Petrov was the Soviet at the United Nations who was feeding the FBI information under the watchful eye and ears of the CIA in November 1963. Charlie and Bruce were given his FBI interview after the assassination. His cover was not blown for more than twenty years. He publicly defected in 1986, just before *glasnost* came into full swing.

Many of the calls Charlie made from the Charlotte airport to old Agency friends pointed to Petrov as the person most likely to know about what Charlie was interested in. But they all discouraged him from thinking he would ever get a full and complete answer.

The follow-up calls and visits Charlie made to ex-Agency types in the West Virginia panhandle confirmed that. Billy Mays was the most emphatic. He had been the Soviet Russia Division's principal liaison to the FBI's intelligence people for years. He now ran an antique store in Harpers Ferry. Mary Jane had bought two matching eighteenth-century wing chairs from him. Billy told Charlie that nobody from Our Side ever knew enough to have any more than suspicions that could never be confirmed or eliminated and scrubbed. Charlie asked for names of those on the suspects' list. None of them was Bruce Conn Clark, which in the counterintelligence-Angleton world could mean something terribly important or, on the other hand, absolutely nothing at all.

Charlie was not looking forward to spending a lot of time with Top Hat. He had had his fill of dealing with defectors when he was with the Agency. He never fully trusted, liked or even admired any of the ones he dealt with. Those who said they were doing it for philosophical reasons—the Born Agains, as they were called in the Agency—never quite rang true to Charlie. No matter what they said about the sins of Mother Russia, Godless Czechoslovakia, Repressive East Germany or the glories of Capitalist America, Freedom and Democracy, it came out sounding like memorized answers for a quiz show. He came to simply despise those who did it for money. What kind of person sells out his or her country for a few dollars? If somebody would do it once, wouldn't they sell out their buyers to somebody else? And, of course, there was always the real possibility with every Here-I-Am-America type that he was a setup, a false defector sent by the KGB to plant bad information.

Several weeks after Charlie and Bruce finished their special Kennedy assassination assignment a high-level Soviet KGB agent named Yuri Nosenko defected in Geneva with the story that he had been the KGB man assigned to monitor Lee Harvey Oswald for the twenty months he was in the Soviet Union. Nosenko's story was that not only did the KGB have nothing to do with the assassination but also that they did not recruit Oswald as an agent and did not even really ever interview him to get those big radar-operator secrets. Nosenko said the Soviets thought he was a kook and thus of no value to the KGB. Charlie was one of many CIA people who worked hard to try to establish once and for all what the truth was, but nobody was able to do so. Angleton, for one, went to his grave believing Nosenko was a false defector. There were others in the Agency who felt just as strongly the other way. Charlie tended to agree with Angleton but it was a close call. The internal dispute about it ripped the Soviet-watching elements of the Agency apart and kept it that way for many years. Several careers were ruined or stymied along the way.

Top Hat was considered by most, including Angleton, to be legitimate. The Yorktown man acted as the arranger for Charlie because Top Hat's Agency and FBI handlers wanted as few people as possible to know where the defector now lived. Charlie assumed it was within one hundred miles of Washington because that was the policy. Easy access for one more interview, one more try at bleeding one more drop of blood from the turnip. Turnips were what defectors were called.

The rendezvous spot was not selected by Charlie. It was a cemetery behind a small Episcopal Church in Millwood, a town of antique stores and old houses some thirty minutes south of Charles Town just below Berryville, Virginia. The time was eleven o'clock on Tuesday morning. There had even been an ID exchange worked out.

Charlie came six minutes early, but Petrov was already there, leaning on a headstone way in the back of the cemetery. Two other men sat in a black Mercury sedan in the church's small parking lot. They were obviously Petrov's "baby-sitters" from the FBI. There was an unspoken informal agreement that neither the Americans nor the Soviets would murder each other's defectors in his or her own new country. It came into being after Anthony Blunt's friends Burgess and Maclean and then Philby went to Moscow. There were many intelligence officers in the United States as well as Britain who were pushing for permission to mount extermination projects against those three as a form of deterrence for other would-be-runaways or defectors if nothing else. The Russians found out about those possibilities, of course, and the deal was struck. But the CIA and the FBI could never fully count on the deal holding. Policies like that can change overnight with the wind and with the defector, and the last thing the United States needed was for some unprotected Soviet defector to turn up on a Virginia backroad with a bullet in his head. That would be bad for business.

"Good morning," said Charlie to Petrov. "This is a place of peace."

"Do you have ancestors buried here?" Petrov replied.

Charlie racked his memory of sounds to see if he recognized the voice from that Agency wire-tap recording on November 22, 1963. It was the same voice but it had learned to speak English much better.

"Not yet," he said to Petrov.

That was the prearranged identification exchange Charlie had worked out with the Yorktown man. Petrov, gray-haired with a round smiling face, extended his right hand. Charlie took it and shook it.

"Mr. Henderson," said Petrov.

"Yes," Charlie said. Petrov spoke English with only a trace of an accent. He was dressed in a well-cut dark gray sport coat, charcoal-brown woolen slacks and a maroon turtleneck shirt. His shoes were shiny black loafers with tassels. This wardrobe, thought Charlie, was his courtesy of United States taxpayers. The sight of it on him triggered all of Charlie's prejudices against turnips.

"There is a bench over there," Petrov said. Charlie followed him to the concrete bench that appeared to have been there as long as most of the graves, which the headstones dated from the late eighteenth and early nineteenth centuries.

"I cannot imagine that there is one thing left in my mind to say about anything," Petrov said after they were seated and facing each other at half-angles.

To the casual observer they would have appeared to be two old men of bearing and taste talking probably about old times in the company of an ancestor who was buried there in that cemetery. It was a perfect October day, cool enough for coats, warm enough not to shiver. The trees throughout and around the small cemetery still had some color. And there was a smell and sound of leaves.

"My questions are few and very specific," Charlie said. "Maybe you cannot help me, but I thought it was worth a try."

"Why, certainly," said Petrov. "Your country has been very good to me, so whatever I can do in exchange is . . . how do you say, 'A-OK' with me." Charlie hated people of all nationalities who said "how do you say . . ." before saying something in English or any other language.

Charlie had absolutely no desire to make small talk with this guy, so he got on with it.

"I am interested in pursuing a line of questioning that your debriefers have already gone over with you in detail," he said.

"And that is the fact that there was a Soviet agent in the highest levels of the U.S. government during the seventies."

Petrov closed his eyes and shook his head. "Oh, please, Mr. Henderson, not again," he said. "I do not exaggerate when I say I have spent thousands of hours and millions of minutes talking about this. There is *glasnost* and *perestroika* now, our countries are friends, whoever this person was is no longer spying for Russia. Why not, how you say, let . . ."

"Let sleeping dogs lie?"

"Yes, that is it."

"How do you know he is no longer spying?"

"Because he stopped."

"When?"

"In 1980."

"Exactly when?"

"I don't know exactly when. Please. I have been over and over this so many times."

"Good, then one more time should not be that big of an imposition." Charlie did not give a damn what this guy wanted. We the Taxpayers of the United States of America own you, Petrov, and I am a Taxpayer and you will talk to me as long as I want to talk to you. "How many people on the Soviet side knew the identity of this American?" Charlie asked.

"Very few. It was the highest-held secret there was. I am not sure if even the head of the KGB knew for sure. It was all done through what you people call cutouts."

"Explain that, please." Charlie saw the tired frown come to Petrov's face. "One more time."

"Okay," said Petrov. "No Soviet ever talked or communicated in any way with this American. It was the only operation I ever saw or heard of that had three, sometimes four, how do you say . . ."

"Cutouts. You just said it yourself."

"Yes, cutouts. An American, also working for us—us, the Soviets—would make the pickup. He would pass it on to another American who would pass it on to someone else, maybe a Czech or sometimes even a Yugoslav who worked for us. It was washed and dried many times before it got to KGB. I think even then most of the contact was made through dead drops. You know how that works . . ."

"I know about dead drops, thanks. Why such an elaborate system?"

"Because this man, whoever he was, was so big and important. He should never be in jeopardy from defection or anything else."

"That was a wise move," Charlie said. "If you had known, for instance, you would have told us."

"That is correct, Mr. Henderson. That is correct."

"What kind of information did this man turn over?"

"That I do not know. What I do know, what I have told you now and what I have told so many others before, is all information that came to me accidentally from friends and fellow workers. I was never officially involved in the operation with this big and important American. Never, was I."

"Was he paid?"

"I was told he was not but I do not know for sure."

"What were you told?"

"That he did it for love."

"Love of whom or what?"

"I have no idea. Maybe a woman? Maybe an idea? Maybe, maybe, maybe? I do not know."

Charlie cleared his throat, looked over at a tall, stately sycamore tree that was shedding its leaves like they were brown snowflakes. The time had come to ask the real question he had come to ask.

"Based on what you know of the system over there," he said, "is it likely that anything was written down about the KGB relationship with this big and important American?"

"Of that I am sure. Certainly. The KGB does not twist a paper-clip into a long piece of wire without writing it down."

Neither does the CIA, thought Charlie. The problem—sometimes a good problem—is finding the piece or pieces of paper it was written down on.

"So there is a file somewhere in Moscow with the details of this?" Charlie asked.

"I have never seen such a file and I do not know for a fact, but I believe it is most likely, most likely there is such a file. Most likely. Unless somebody destroyed it, of course."

"Who would destroy it?"

Petrov shrugged to the heavens. "Ask the God in the American heavens, do not ask me. This is all, how do you say, guess . . ."

"Guesswork?"

"Yes, guesswork."

"One more piece of guesswork, Mr. Petrov, and then you can go back to your tailors or wherever."

"Tailors? I do not go to tailors. I go to Neiman-Marcus."

"Never mind. If you had to guess about whether this file or whether the identity of this man will ever get out, what would you say?"

Petrov looked away for a few seconds. This was clearly heavy guesswork, thought Charlie.

"My guesswork on this is yes. Yes, it will eventually be known. I believe, as I am sure you believe, that eventually everything is known. Eventually it will become to somebody's interest to tell. Secrets are like meat; they can be frozen or eaten but not kept."

Charlie stood up but did not extend his right hand. "Thank you for coming. Just put it on the tab."

Petrov was on his feet now. "The tab? I do not understand."

"It was a very small joke."

Petrov laughed. "I love your American jokes."

They walked together to the parking lot. Alexander Gannady Petrov got into the backseat of the black Mercury and rode off.

Charlie followed them a few seconds later in his Wagoneer. He was thinking mostly about love.

The call from Jay Buckner came in the afternoon. Bruce took it immediately and almost with a sense of relief.

"Henderson's up to something," Jay said. "But I don't know what. He's been talking to all kinds of ex-Agency types around here. He even made a couple of passes at the guys at the fisheries. I sold them their houses, so I act as a kind of town crier among 'em. Don't know what it's all about."

"Did you say the fisheries?"

"Yeah. There's a federal fisheries between Charles Town and Shepherdstown. Labs and things. The Agency keeps some houses up behind it to do some of its own experimenting."

Bruce was curious about what kind of experiments they might be. Maybe they were still working on ways to kill Castro. Maybe they were going to try it with arsenic-laced filet of halibut or try to put a poison dart in a can of tuna.

But he was not curious enough to ask Buckner a follow-up question. Instead, he said, "What kinds of questions is he asking?"

"Oh, they were mostly about that old saw about the mole in the high levels of government," Jay said. "Most everyone thought it was Angleton bullshit, but we heard it all of the time. Everybody heard it all of the time. He was also trying to get a lead on a Russkie defector the FBI has put up somewhere down in Virginia."

"Did he find him?"

"Don't know."

"Who was he?"

"I think it was Petrov. The U.N. guy all of the stink was made about when he went public and came over a few years ago."

"I appreciate your checking in, Jaybird."

"Still don't need me, Brucebear?"

The question of what he needed now triggered Bruce to respond spontaneously: "Yes, as a matter of fact, I do need you, Jaybird. Could you come down here to see me in a day or two? I would want to talk about it in person."

"Just name the time and the place."

Bruce looked at his carefully prepared appointment book and then named a time and a place.

━━━━━━━━━━

Fourteen days had passed since Charlie had run into Bruce Conn Clark at DeCarlo's. Two weeks of old times' excitement and danger, of new times' heavy breathing and thinking.

Now, two days after his cemetery meeting with Petrov, as he walked the railroad track by himself, it was down only to the thinking. He had himself a theory about Bruce. The man was a traitor. The Soviets, after first hitting up his brother on the Kennedy assassination, came back. When? Maybe the next week, maybe ten years later, maybe twenty years later. But they came back. Particularly, they came back when he was secretary of state. Think about it. The secretary of state of the United States working for the other side!

Incredible.

It sure as hell would explain why Bruce Conn Clark moved so quickly and so roughly against Charlie to stop the ball of yarn from unwinding. Bruce would wake up every day from then on wondering if it was the one that would bring the call from the reporter in Moscow. "Mr. Clark, this is Adams of the AP in Moscow. There's an ex-KGB type who has come to us with a document that says you were a spy for them. That can't be true, sir, can it?" Or the call could come from someone at the Agency or, more probably, from the White House or the State Department. "One of Gorbachev's people has just informed us they have a file back in Moscow that proves you, sir, worked for them while you were secretary of state. They say that unless we agree to what they want on a new aid package, then out it comes. What is this all about, sir?" Maybe because it involved Clark the call might be made by the president or the current secretary of state.

Incredible.

Maybe—hopefully—the Angleton thesis about the obvious was true again. Only in reverse. Maybe it only seems like Bruce Conn Clark was a spy. Maybe there is another explanation. Maybe somebody wants me to think he is. Maybe the obvious is too obvious. Maybe, maybe, maybe. Unfortunately there was only one way to find out for sure. He wished there was somebody to talk it over with. Josh? No way. He's still there. He would have to do something and whatever he did would mean the shaking of mountains and monuments all over Washington.

Well, then, why not Mary Jane? Damn it, yes. Mary Jane, here I come.

Finally.

He turned back toward the road and walked so fast and so intently that he barely noticed what he always noticed on his walks. The sounds and sights of birds, trees and other living natural things.

———————

Bruce decided the best place to have the most important conversation of his life was at his apartment. He set the time for early afternoon so Jay could go back to West Virginia on the train if he wished.

"I want to hire you," Bruce said to Jay. They were sitting side by side on the leather couch.

Bruce handed Jay a white envelope. Jay took it, opened it. Inside were sixty one-thousand-dollar bills.

"You into drug running or something, Brucebear?" said Buckner, tossing the envelope down on the space between them. "Only druggies deal in cash like that."

"No, Jaybird, I want you to commit a murder."

Jay blinked, shook his head. "I took on that business with Charlie Henderson for old times' sake," he said. "But I am not a hired killer. All the killing I have ever done was either in self-defense or in the name of the security of my nation. I sell real estate."

"I know," said Bruce. "But this killing is special."

"Not Charlie, I hope."

"Not Charlie."

"Tell me who, then, and I will decide if it's special enough."

"Me. I want you to murder me."

Jay picked up the envelope and tossed it across the room at the desk, the one Bruce had sat at when he tore up the invitations and talked to the telephone information operator.

"Forget it, Brucebear. If you want to die, kill yourself." He got to his feet. "I'm out of here."

"Sit down and hear me out."

"I will not have a conversation about killing you. I am not in the suicide-for-hire business either, old buddy. You are Bruce Conn Clark, former secretary of state and prominent man of the nation and the world. You have no reason to die. I'm leaving. Unless you are an Agency real estate buyer or appraiser or you are interested in buying an old English manor house on two hundred twenty acres that could easily be converted to a horse farm or a bed-and-breakfast or something like that, forget another second of conversation."

Bruce followed Jay toward the front door of the apartment. "What if I told you I had a terminal disease?" Bruce said.

"I'd say, okay, hang in there awhile and it will do the job for you."

"Maybe I don't want to suffer, maybe I would rather go quickly and cleanly now."

"Then maybe you go buy you a pistol and some ammo, load up and stick the barrel in your mouth and pull the trigger. If that's too messy, then maybe you get some doctor to give you a big prescription of sleeping pills or you throw yourself down in front of the local to Martinsburg or whatever. But just don't talk to me about it."

"Jay, please, sit down. Hear me out. One more minute."

Jay had his hand on the doorknob. "You've got a minute. I am counting. One hundred and one, one hundred and two, one hundred and three . . ."

"I don't want to go out a suicide, Jay. I don't want to be remembered for the way I died rather than what I did when I was alive. Please, Jay."

Jay sighed. "I'll think about it. What disease is it you have anyhow?"

"Cancer," Bruce said.

"What kind?"

"Colon. Colon cancer."

"Sure. I'll be in touch." Jay opened the door.

"When?"

"When I have something to say."

"Close the door," Bruce said. Jay closed the door. Bruce continued: "If you decide to do it don't tell me about it, just go and do it. Just kill me. That way it will look authentic. Make it look like a robbery, a random crime. I won't want the police to be around looking for special or strange motives."

"What are you talking about?"

"Nothing. Please, do your best to make it look like a random killing. Somebody who did not know me killed me for my watch, not because of who I am or what I am—or was."

"Anything you say, Brucebear."

———

They talked over dinner downstairs and then, for most of the rest of the night, in their upstairs sitting room sipping Calvados, Charlie's favorite after-dinner drink. He acquired a taste for it while stationed covertly as an AT&T sales representative in Paris in the late 1970s. The best thing that came with the assignment was a terrific apartment on the Ile St-Louis that was appropriate for his status as a well-situated American business executive living abroad.

Only Charlie talked for the first two hours or so. Mary Jane listened in a state of silent surprise while her husband told her what he had been doing for the last fourteen days and why he had been doing it. He began at the beginning, with his and Bruce's Kennedy assassination assignment.

Mary Jane began responding before he got to the absolute end. "Why did you go to South Carolina?" she asked. "What was the point of that?"

"I wanted to talk to the brother, to pick and putter around. Who knows? I thought there was a connection between the brother and Bruce's crazy reaction to me, to having Buckner go after me and all, but I did not know exactly what it was. I didn't count on Bruce getting onto me so fast and, of course, I didn't count on the brother's being unable to talk."

"What did you do with the BB gun, Charlie?"

"Threw it out of the car on the way back to the airport. I knew I couldn't get it through airport security. Easy come, easy go."

"We could have used it on the groundhogs and snakes here," Mary Jane said. "Did you ever kill anybody when you were with the Agency?"

They were upstairs and well into the Calvados by now. Charlie topped off their small glasses with a touch more.

"No, my darling, I did not. We went through that with the kids. I was a covert operator, not an assassin, for Christ's sake."

"Where did you learn to use weapons like a BB pistol or whatever it was?"

"I was trained to use a gun and I carried one several times. But I never killed anybody. Would it bother you if I did? Remember what I was fighting was a war. A war with an enemy that looks meek and mild and incompetent and over the hill now, but he didn't look that way in my time. No, ma'am. He did not."

"There were many times when you were gone when I wondered if you were out there trying to murder Castro or Khrushchev and people like that. I hated to think that I was married to somebody who killed people for a living."

"Would you have felt the same way if I was a marine officer or a D.C. cop?"

"That's different."

"No, it isn't."

"Why didn't your people at the CIA know how tender and vulnerable all of that Communist world was? One huff and one puff and down it all came in Eastern Europe and in the Soviet Union. Why were we Americans all so surprised?"

" 'Your people,' meaning me? No comment."

"Come on, Charlie. If we're going to talk, let's talk. Let's talk about everything."

Okay, what the hell? He said: "To tell you the truth, I am as mystified as anybody. I was as surprised as anybody. And I spent thirty-four years working in the business of finding out and knowing about those bastards. I had no idea it was such a house of cards. I hate to admit it but that is the fact."

"Don't be personal, Charlie. I didn't mean it personally."

"It is personal. I think it was because we all saw it as a game. I loved playing it. You either love it or get out of it. Nobody plays it half-assed. You either get burned or killed or fired or all three in quick-quick hurry. I think we were all like the big-time college football team that cared only about the score and nothing about our classes or anything else at school. Can we go back to Bruce Conn Clark? The reason we're talking, remember, is because I have to decide what to do about what I believe about this man."

She waved him on. And he repeated what he had said before she asked about the South Carolina trip. Most of it had to do with his conversations the last couple of days with former Agency people and Top Hat.

"Like I say, the result is I believe Clark was blackmailed into spying for the Soviet Union. He did it to save his brother's reputation and his own career and ass. For brotherly love and love of himself."

Mary Jane poured them both more Calvados. "I think that has to be wrong, Charlie. It just does not seem right that a secretary of state could be a spy. It really doesn't."

Charlie suddenly wished he had not told her a thing. He didn't want anybody to argue with him, particularly an amateur. Even if that amateur was his wife, somebody he loved dearly, she was still an amateur.

But he went through his thesis again, dotting what further *i*'s he could. Mary Jane sat more quietly this time. Charlie couldn't tell if it was because she was digesting what he was saying or because the Calvados had turned her off.

The Calvados was beginning to make a difference in his thinking and his talking. Both were slurred. Both were sloppy.

"The question is, what I should do about it?" he said.

"Why do anything?" Mary Jane replied. The Calvados was getting to her a bit, too.

"Because it is—or would be—the biggest U.S. spy case in history, that is why. For a man like Bruce Conn Clark to sell out his country . . ."

"You said he was blackmailed. Did he take money?"

"I don't think so. But he still sold out."

"To save a brother is a lot different than taking money, Charlie. They are not both selling out."

Damn it! "Believe me, they are the same," he said.

"They are not."

"Well, either way, the world should know."

"Why?"

"Goddamn it, Mary Jane, because they should. The American world in particular."

"How old is he?"

"Same as me and you. Maybe a little older."

"He doesn't spy anymore, does he?"

"Probably not, but that's only because he doesn't know anything anymore."

"Why ruin his reputation now? All of that awful stuff is behind him. Why not let it all, you know, just kind of lie there unknown and unacted upon?"

"I could be known as the great spycatcher, the man who unmasked Bruce Conn Clark as the ultimate master Soviet spy of history. Isn't that worth something?"

"Is it to you?"

The Calvados had taken complete hold of Charlie now. There were three Mary Janes sitting across from him on the flowered chair that now had three times as many flowers on its covering. The small light hanging from the ceiling had become three lights.

Charlie closed his eyes and passed out.

"We'll talk about this some more in the morning," said Mary Jane. It wasn't long before she closed her eyes, too.

———————

Bruce went through his day expecting to be killed.

He awoke thinking Jay would come bursting into the apartment any minute. He would probably be wearing a ski mask and sneakers, using a pistol with a silencer. He would shoot him, making it look like a robbery. God, be quick. Hit the heart or the brain or something that made it be quick.

But nothing happened. And, like any other day, soon he had his muffin—it was a blueberry bran—with orange juice and decaf coffee and he was dressed.

Maybe he's waiting in the hallway. Or in the elevator.

But no. There was nobody in either except the usual people, and in a few minutes he was crossing the Watergate lobby. His car and driver were outside. He could see them through the door. A sniper shot would be perfect. From the Howard Johnson's across the street? Perfect. A second Watergate scandal featuring the same two buildings!

No shots rang out from the Howard Johnson's. Also, no man in a ski mask came up to the car and stuck a pistol in his ribs and demanded his billfold and his watch.

Well. Would it make sense to do it on the drive to the office? Maybe here at the intersection of Virginia and New Hampshire avenues. We're stopped for a light. Right. I could be pulled out of the backseat and shot. Probably not. That is the way political assassins operate, not armed robbers.

The driver, a new man whose name was Richard, dropped Bruce at the K Street entrance of the building. No one was lying in wait. Bruce walked through the lobby and rode the elevator up to the offices of Clark and Associates on the eighth floor without incident and unscathed.

Damn!

The blue folder held out the prospect of a typically busy and routine day. There were two client meetings in the morning, two more in the afternoon, lunch at the Metropolitan Club with an old friend, Stan Rosenfield, and many phone calls and letter signings in between. The only chance for Jay would be lunch. Bruce would walk the four blocks to the Metropolitan Club. That could set up a good, clean street robbery. In broad daylight. Perfect. A street robbery. A lot of yelling and screaming from passersby about "Stop that man!" And then somebody, maybe a young lawyer with a flair for remembering famous faces, would look down at the dead man on the street and announce: "Holy shit! It's Bruce Conn Clark!" Or something like that.

There was no attack on the walk over. The lunch with Stan, as always, was terrific. Stan had been Bruce's special Middle East negotiator. In earlier Democratic administrations he had been the United States ambassador to Spain and to the OAS, and he did a lot of other good and useful things for his government, like help negotiate the Panama Canal treaty. Now, like Bruce, he was left out in the cold by succeeding Republican administrations. But it never seemed to bother Stan, who mostly went about his business of practicing law, serving on corporate and think-tank boards and staying off the TV talk shows on the grounds that they never let him finish a coherent thought. Stan always brought an agenda to his regular lunches with Bruce. Today it was how to get Jim Baker to get the president to understand that Saddam Hussein will never ever back down. Threatening war means going to war. Stan also allowed plenty of time for Bruce to talk about whatever he had on his mind. But this time Bruce had only one thing on his mind and he could not talk about it with Stan. So they talked almost solely about Saddam Hussein and how their many mutual friends and former associates were doing out of government and thus out of the loop.

Stan was a gentle man of integrity and smarts who always left Bruce feeling better. It happened again this day so much so that he had walked almost an entire block before he was reminded of the fact that Jay might be stalking him for the kill.

But he wasn't. And Bruce made it back to the office for the afternoon of quiet, safe labors on behalf of his important and prosperous clients.

At the end of the day he went by two quick in-and-out receptions. One was at the Russell Office Building for a senator who was celebrating the presence of the prime minister of Kenya. The other was at the Madison Hotel in honor of a visiting former foreign minister of Israel.

There were no attempts made on his life going to, during or leaving either function.

That left only dinner. One of the invitations he had torn up while drinking vodka was to go to dinner that night at the Georgetown home of a former Treasury secretary who now represented the interests of various Arab countries. Bruce had also done some work for those countries, but he was glad he was not going there for dinner. He was glad he was not going anywhere for dinner. The car dropped him at the Watergate just after eight o'clock. There were no attempts on his life.

He opened a bottle of Perrier. He was not hungry for anything more. He changed to his pajamas, took a Restoril sleeping pill and picked up a book to read. He kept several on the table by his bed so that he could go with whatever spirit or mood struck him.

Tonight he wanted something light. Someone had given him a paperback copy of a novel called *The White House Mess*. The friend had said that it was about just what the title implied and that it was hilarious.

No offense to the author, but Bruce could read only the first twenty-five pages before he was asleep. Expecting death all day had worn him out.

━━━━━━━━

The taste of Calvados was in his mouth, stomach and head but he had to move. He had an appointment in Shepherdstown at ten with Mathews and Shanks, a classy antique store run by Joe Mathews and John Shanks. Robert, their workshop man, was trying to make something of an old chair Mary Jane had picked up at the Middleway flea market. Joe and John wanted to show Charlie what had to be done before they did it.

Mary Jane was awake but also in Calvados pain. Charlie dressed quickly, brought her a cup of coffee and raced out of the house. "I may walk the canal afterward," he said to her. There was no reply.

The canal was the C and O Canal, a monument to a failure in America's industrial transportation past that had lived on as something quite different and successful. President John Quincy Adams compared it to the pyramids of Egypt and the Colossus of Rhodes when he turned the first spadeful of dirt on July 4, 1828. The original idea was for a canal that went from Pittsburgh and the Ohio River alongside the Potomac River through Washington, D.C., to the Chesapeake Bay and the Atlantic Ocean. After twenty-two years of digging it had gone from Washington to Cumberland, Maryland, a distance of 184 miles. And that was as far as it ever went. The idea was to bring coal and steel to the Atlantic for shipment all over the world. But the railroads were also building along the same route to do the same thing. A race to complete ended in a rout. The railroads were operating eight years before the canal. But barge traffic did operate through its seventy-five locks until 1924, when it was shut down for good. It has sat there mostly undisturbed except by the weather as a national park for hikers and bicyclists ever since. In Washington its towpath is a favorite place for joggers and dog exercisers, and on spring Sundays it can be as crowded as a shopping mall. But the farther you go, the fewer people there are and the more wonderful it is.

It took only a few minutes to do his business with Mathews and Shanks, and he was on the canal before eleven. The way on at Shepherdstown was under the bridge on the road to Sharpsburg and Antietam. Charlie parked the Wagoneer in the small lot at the old lock there and started to walk northwest on the towpath.

The Potomac was on the left, quiet, full and tranquil, the unused ditch of the canal on the right. Charlie had walked it hundreds of times, but it always seemed to be better than the last time. It was maybe 60 degrees and there was a little sun, perfect for a good walk.

He walked a steady pace for twenty-five minutes, saw not one fellow human and stopped. He took some deep breaths, imagined that he no longer tasted Calvados in his mouth, stomach and head and started back to the parking lot.

Ten minutes or so later he saw a figure some fifty yards ahead on the left side of the path in front of him. As he got closer he realized casually that it was a man. A fisherman, he assumed.

It was not until he was almost on the man that he recognized him. It was Jay Buckner.

Well, well, thought Charlie. So here is where it ends for Charles Avenue Henderson of Joplin, Missouri, age sixty-four, on the towpath of the C and O Canal just above Lock 38.

There was no point in running, grabbing a stick or anything like that. Buckner had been well trained by the government of the United States of America to come fully prepared and equipped for missions of this type.

"Hi, Charlie," Jay said.

Charlie put his hands up over his head as if surrendering. "Take me, I'm yours."

"I'm in real estate, Charlie," Jay said. "Put your goddamn hands down."

Charlie put his goddamn hands down. "I already own a house," he said. "I can't help you on moving the Agency up here. I think it's a bad idea . . ."

"I want to tell you a story about Bruce Conn Clark," Buckner said. "It's a short story. It goes like this: Once upon a time two days ago he asked me to come see him in Washington. I did. He asked me to kill him. He said he had terminal cancer. Cancer of the colon. It didn't sound right so I had an old acquaintance in the Agency's medical department check it out with Bruce's doctor. The cancer story was bullshit. He had a full physical three months ago and he was in perfect health. So I wondered what in the hell is going on. And that is why I took the liberty of coming here for a chat with you."

"Forget it, Buckner. I don't talk to people who put bombs in my hotel rooms and cut steering wires and do other nasty things to my cars and person."

"You are standing here, aren't you?"

"No thanks to you."

"Bullshit, Charlie. With all thanks to me. I worked as hard as I have ever worked on all of those damned things to make sure you didn't die. Bruce wanted you scared. He said you were blackmailing him."

"Now, that is real bullshit."

"Whatever, you are alive, thanks to me."

Charlie came close to laughing out loud. "The logic of that is off the wall, asshole."

"Men our age, we the grandfathers, should not be using the language we do," Buckner said. "Why does Bruce Conn Clark want to die? is the question. And I have a hunch you know the answer."

"No comment."

" 'No comment' is the answer of a real asshole."

"I have nothing to say to you about anything concerning Bruce Conn Clark. Period, end of statement, end of interview."

Charlie began to move. It was his moment of truth for the morning. Would Jay Buckner stand aside and let him pass on to the rest of his natural life or did he have other plans?

Jay gave way. Slightly. "Let me ask you one question, then, Charlie. Should I kill him?"

"What?"

"You heard me. Should I kill him?"

"I repeat. What?"

"Based on what you know, does he deserve to die? That is another way of putting the question."

Charlie's mind and legs froze. "I don't know," he said after a few beats of silence. "Maybe he does."

"Maybe isn't good enough."

Charlie made a decision. "Don't kill him. Not now, at least. Give me some time to think."

"It's yours. You have my number."

Yes, sir. I have your number, all right.

Charlie decided to stop at his favorite local restaurant, The Yellow Brick Bank in Shepherdstown, before heading back to Charles Town. He wanted a bowl of their black bean soup, a glass of cold white wine and some time.

———

Mary Jane was down at the tennis court when Charlie got back. She was pounding ball after ball from her ball machine. Charlie

watched for a minute, noticing that she had the machine programmed for her to hit the ball at a safe slow speed at one place.
So she didn't have to move or strain. Just hit the ball as hard as she
could.

She turned off the machine and came over to Charlie. Her face,
always alive and young, seemed dead and old. The Calvados had
done even more damage to her than to him.

Standing there on the court, Charlie told her what Jay Buckner
had said.

"What is the answer, Charlie?" she said after a while. "Does he
deserve to die?"

If Charlie knew the answer to that he would not have brought
it up. "What do you think, sweetheart?" he said.

"I think the American system does not allow for individuals to
be the judge, jury and executioner."

"Oh, come on, Mary Jane. That is not the issue here."

"It sure is."

"It's a form of suicide. He's asked Buckner to kill him because
he can't do it himself. That's all there is to it."

" 'All'? What do you mean, 'all'?"

"I mean he knows he's going to be exposed as a goddamn traitor
to his country either by me or somebody else. And he doesn't want
to be around to see it. It seems to me like a justifiable reason for
suicide—if there is such a thing."

"Exactly."

"Exactly what?"

"There isn't. Go talk to him. Confront him. Tell him it's not
worth dying over. You owe him that."

"The man's a goddamn traitor. I don't owe him a thing."

"You think he's a traitor. You don't know that for sure. Can you
really prove it?"

Charlie leaned down and picked up one of the many yellow
tennis balls lying around on the court. He threw it like a baseball
hard against a faraway fence.

Lucy DeCarlo, happy to see them again, gave them a corner table in the back room and kept other people away to protect their privacy.

"It's hard to believe it was eighteen days ago that this all began right here," said Charlie to Bruce.

"It seems like eighteen years," Bruce replied.

Bruce joined Charlie in ordering a glass of red wine, a Chianti. And he ordered a full meal, an agnolotti first course, a filet of sole dish called *Sogliola alla Boscaiola* and the house salad. Charlie had the Caesar salad and the veal parmigiana with linguine on the side.

They had a lot to say to each other, and since the dinner was at Charlie's invitation he started it.

"Buckner told me you asked him to kill you," he said. "He figured out your cancer lie and assumed it had something to do with me. His question was simply, does Bruce Conn Clark deserve to die?"

Charlie looked right at Bruce and took a sip of wine.

"How did you answer it?" Bruce said.

"I haven't yet. That is why we are here."

"Obviously that is why I am still able to be here, too," Bruce said. "I have been expecting the sound of gunfire for three days."

"Do you deserve to die, Bruce Conn Clark?"

Bruce was not absolutely sure what Charlie had in mind to talk about at dinner. This particular question was not one he expected to be asked. Not like this. Not so early in dinner. Not so right between the eyes.

"No," said Bruce, "if you put it like that. I do not deserve to die. But I must."

"Traitors deserve to die. It's the law of the land."

Bruce had a bite of his salad and a third gulp of his wine. "I am not prepared to admit that I am a traitor."

"What were you, then?"

"If I tell you, what happens, Charlie? What do you do with my story? Who do you tell it to? Our Kennedy assassination story was a molehill compared to this. My story is a mountain. It could turn you into a national hero, maybe. Is that what you want to be, Charlie?"

"This is about you, not me."

"Bullshit."

Bullshit is right, thought Charlie. "What kind of ground rules do you want?"

"Only one," Bruce said. "That you never tell anyone before I die and not even after I die unless it comes out somewhere else first. Then, if you want to jump on the grave, participate in the piling on of my disgraced corpse, go right ahead."

"No deal."

"No story."

"I have enough already to get something started."

"You don't have a thing but a lot of guesses."

"You were a mole, Mr. Bruce Conn Clark. The Russians came back to your brother and through him they got to you. That is the reason you came after me so hard with Buckner. You have a helluva lot more to protect than that Kennedy assassination thing. You goddamn lied when you told me in South Carolina they never came back. They always came back. Always. Particularly when the asset becomes the secretary of state of the United States of America."

"You cannot prove that."

"I can smell it. I'll leave it to others to prove."

They were both breathing hard. The second courses arrived and each took several bites in silence.

Charlie had no idea where he was headed.

Neither did Bruce.

It was Charlie who finally got them talking again. But about something else.

"I didn't know until the other day that you were a Blue Heart," he said.

"Took a shot from a guy in Portugal," Bruce said. "It wasn't that big a deal."

"Blue Hearts are always big deals."

"Maybe so."

Bruce tore off a piece of Italian bread and buttered it. He seldom put butter on his bread, but all of that didn't seem important anymore. He said, "How about going back to the business at hand?"

Charlie said, "Okay. I don't think I have to remind you that I am holding the cards in this game. You have nothing going for you."

"That's true. Except maybe the hope that you are a decent man."

"Oh, spare me that, please. It is hard to be a decent man to somebody who gave secrets to the enemy, who has had somebody put a bomb in his hotel room . . ."

Bruce held up both hands. "All right, all right, all right. I came here tonight to tell you what happened. It is a story that is embedded in my soul, in my heart, in my very being. I have never ever talked about it with anyone. Not one person. I tried to work a deal, you said forget it. So, that is that. My only hope now is to tell you the truth so you will understand why I must die and why you must tell Jay Buckner to do it. So shut up and listen. If you take it and make yourself a hero instead, then so be it. I can't do a damned thing about it. You are right. You have the cards."

Their main courses were now on the table. But neither took a bite or even looked down at them.

Bruce said: "Yes, Charlie, the Russians came back. Twelve years after the Kennedy assassination they came again to Duane with that half of the queen of hearts. I was by then on the National Security Council staff. The proposition they put to Duane was similar to the one you just put to me. We have this card and all other cards, they said. Your brother cooperates with us or we blow you and him. We get the story out about your association with Anthony Blunt at Cambridge and maybe even how we used the Clark brothers to sit on the allegation that the Soviet Union was behind the Kennedy assassination. They promised top-level handling, airtight security and anything else we wanted—including money. I took the deal without the money. I felt I had no choice. I was on the fast track to who knows where and I also felt— correctly, I might add—that I was smarter than they were and that I could handle it in such a way that nobody would get hurt. Including my country, the United States of America. And that is what happened. I fed them information, information that was irrelevant or slightly wrong. They took it and loved it. When I was secretary of state it was almost a blessing because I had two channels to the highest levels of the Soviet Union. One from the top down, another from the bottom. I used them well to get done what was in the best interests of our country and peace in the world. At no time did I give away an intelligence or military or any other kind of governmental secret that jeopardized lives or even political or diplomatic positions of our government. I was not a traitor. I was smarter than they were, and as a result what I did helped our country, not hurt it. But I know that no one will buy that explanation, particularly if it was spread over the front pages of *The Washington Post* and *The New York Times* and the nightly news programs. I would be marked a spy, a collaborator, a traitor, and that would be the way I would be buried and remembered now and forever more. My harsh reaction to what you said here eighteen nights ago was simply the fact that you could destroy me. I have not handled it well, that is for sure. But that was what it is all about. You guessed right. The fact is that it was all a holding action. And I know that. As the U.S.-Soviet relationship warms and cuddles, there will be some opening of some files in Moscow. Were Julius and Ethel Rosenberg really spies? How about Alger Hiss? That will lead to similar revelations about others. And I am sure there is a piece of paper, probably thousands of pieces of paper, somewhere in the Kremlin that will implicate me. All I was trying to do was buy some time until Duane and I were gone. You could have speeded things up. I tried to stop you and I failed."

He shrugged. He had come to the end of his story.

Charlie had not expected something like this. What did he expect? Who knows? He decided to eat his veal parmigiana. Bruce took a bite of his fish.

"At least you weren't Angleton's Agency mole," Charlie said. "Were you?"

"No!"

"The little things. Thank God for them. I might have had to ask Jay Buckner to kill you and he would probably have done it free of charge if you had been."

They ate some more.

"Some trade-craft questions?" Charlie said. "Like how did you get the stuff to them?"

Bruce smiled for the first time since they sat down at the table. "Oh, Charlie, as a professional you will be impressed. It was a system I designed and insisted on myself. I had only one cutout. My brother Duane. I passed on whatever I had to him in the course of normal contact any normal person would have with his brother. I never ever set an eye on a Soviet 'control.' I designed the system with two other sets of padding. Duane used only other Americans or non-Russians as his contacts, who in turn dropped the merchandise off in dead drops. It would have taken an enormous effort or a leak or a tremendous piece of luck for anyone to have traced anything back to me."

"Who made the contact with your brother in the first place?"

"A drop-in. A Soviet who came into the country for that purpose alone. They knew they were dealing with hot stuff so they decided not to risk the possibility that their regular controls were either under surveillance or turned."

"What kind of things did you give them?"

"No debriefings, please. I have told you how I worked it. Because of my expert training in the Agency and my experience in the Division, I was in good shape to tell them what they wanted to hear without telling them anything. I know it's hard to believe, but that is what happened. The fact that I got away with it for so long is amazing."

"Double amazing. You got away with it with them and with us." Saying those words put Charlie's mind to working.

They ate some more.

Both declined dessert. Both took decaffeinated espresso.

"May I make a summary to the jury?" Bruce said. They had met at seven-thirty. It was now almost ten. There weren't many people left in the restaurant. Spring Valley is an early-to-bed section of Washington.

Charlie nodded.

"I do not want to be around when this story gets out. I could not handle it. But if I kill myself, everybody will ask why. Why did Bruce Conn Clark, the man who has always had everything, take his own golden life? I also do not want to be remembered for being a suicide. Also, and I know this is a thin reed, there is always the possibility that the conservatives will revolt against Gorbachev, *perestroika* and the New World Order will go down the toilet and those files about me in the Kremlin will not get released. Being murdered by a random armed robber or mugger preserves the way of my going and thus my public record. I know that sounds strange but that is important to me."

"It doesn't sound strange at all, damn it," said Charlie with some feeling. "You were ahead of me but my being upset with what had happened to Jack Douglas would probably have gotten around to me and our assassination story. Why shouldn't people know about it now? That would have been the question. I think I know how I would have answered it. You were right."

They fell silent again.

Finally, Bruce said: "Are you going to make a decision sitting right here tonight over decaf espresso or will you call me or drop me a line or will I know it if I hear a shot ring out?"

"May I make a summary statement?"

"Please, Charlie. By all means."

"I am not going to tell Jay Buckner you deserve to die. I am not willing to be your executioner as well as judge and jury. My wife, Mary Jane, convinced me of that. You should know, by the way, that I did tell her about all of this. I had to. But forget my dropping my arm on you like the emperor did on the Christians. If Jay hits you he will do it on his own hook, not mine. My problem has to do with knowing, goddamn it, that you collaborated with the enemy, an enemy that I worked my ass off for thirty-four years to combat. Every nerve in my body tells me to call Josh Bennett at the Agency or somebody else and say, Bruce Conn Clark spied for the Soviet Union. Sic 'em! Let you go into a courtroom and make your defense, make your argument that you never really told them anything important. That is not my job to resolve that. We have a system for that kind of thing. That is not my problem."

"So what happens next?" Bruce said.

"I don't know."

"What if I went to the phone now and told Jay Buckner that I have changed my mind. Kill Charlie Henderson instead. That would solve your problem. Maybe if I told him to expedite it he could have you down before you could sound a really loud alarm with Bennett or anyone else."

"Maybe." Charlie asked, "Is that a threat?"

"Yes," said Bruce with firmness.

"So?"

"So here we sit like the Soviets and the Americans sat for forty years. Each with the power to destroy the other."

"A cold war?"

"Better than a hot one."

"No matter what happens with me you still have to live with the threat from Moscow," Charlie said.

"I have already lived with it for fifteen years. I can handle it a few more, I guess."

"I've got to think about what I am going to do," said Charlie.

"What if I have you killed before you finish your thinking?" Bruce said.

"You would, too, wouldn't you?"

"Wouldn't you if you were in my place?"

"Buckner won't do it for you."

"There are others around."

"Mary Jane knows."

"Two murders for the price of one . . ."

Charlie pushed away from the table and stood up. "I'm getting out of here and away from you. The dinner's on you."

"You need a ride?"

"I drove down from West Virginia and I'm driving back to-night."

"What next, Charlie?"

"I don't know."

He left the table and then marched right back.

"By the way," he said to Bruce. "For the record, I was wrong about Khrushchev. I forgot Dallas was in the Central time zone, an hour behind us in Washington, thirteen hours behind Moscow."

"So Khrushchev ran for cover *after* Kennedy was shot?"

"You got it. So that our final bit of evidence was dead wrong."

Charlie turned again and left the restaurant with such speed that he even forgot to say good night and thanks to Lucy DeCarlo.

═══════════

The wine had given Bruce a slight buzz. The twelve-minute ride in the backseat of the limo to the Watergate went quickly, but when he got there he told the driver to keep going down Virginia Avenue. He did not want to go back to his apartment. Not now, not this minute.

Bruce gave instructions to go left at the light onto New Hamp-shire Avenue to Twenty-fifth Street to M, turn left again and go two blocks. There were three luxury hotels on the corner of M and Twenty-seventh. He decided on The Regent over the Hyatt and the Westin. He told the driver to let him out and said he would catch a taxi home later.

Bruce had been at the opening of The Regent a few years ago. All of Important Washington had been there along with several retired movie stars. It had a different name then and was run by some Asian hotel chain. Bruce had not followed its history since other than to be vaguely aware that it had changed its name and its owners at least twice. It remained a small, elegant hotel that was never crowded.

The bar, as he had hoped, was empty except for a bartender, who Bruce quickly recognized as being Filipino. Good. Filipinos do not feel obligated to entertain their customers with idle chit-chat.

"Sir?" the bartender said to Bruce, who took a seat on one of the padded bar stools. The bar had a pastel Oriental look, with everything in soft blues and browns and chrome. Around on the walls were several, a dozen at least, paintings of flowers.

What to drink?

"A black Russian," Bruce said. It was more than an inside joke for the occasion. That particular after-dinner drink of vodka and Kahlúa over ice had always been his favorite.

And when it was set down in front of him a minute later it looked as good as he remembered it. He held it up as if to toast somebody or some event and drank half of it. He swallowed several times, ran his tongue over the top of his mouth and lifted the glass again. This time when he finished, the glass was empty.

He set it down on the bar. The bartender was there immediately. Neither said anything except with their eyes and smiles. And in less than a minute another black Russian was before Bruce.

This time the bartender, a man of thirty-five or so, did not move quickly away as he had before. Oh, no, don't talk to me, please, thought Bruce.

"Are you not Henry Kissinger?" said the bartender.

"Yes, as a matter of fact, I am," said Bruce. "But please, I beg of you, not to tell anyone."

"Oh, yes, sir. I will not tell a soul."

Bruce downed the second black Russian in two tries again. And again he signaled with his eyes for a third.

"I admire what you have done for the world," said the bartender when he delivered it.

"Thank you," said Bruce.

———————

"This is going to be a tough conversation," Charlie said to Josh Bennett.

They were back on the bench by the fountain in the Tyson's II mall. Charlie had started for home last night, but at the Holiday Inn at Dulles he decided to stop and spend the night. He called Josh at Langley first thing the next morning and here they were a short time later.

"What I am about to say to you, Josh, I would like to be completely unofficial and off the record," Charlie said. "But I realize . . ."

Josh didn't even let him finish. He said: "Forget it, Charlie. Nothing coming my way can ever be unofficial or off the record with me going in. It can't be. After you tell me something I might then decide it can be unofficial and off the record, but not before I know what it is. You tell me somebody is about to blow up Langley at noon . . . well, I have to act on it."

"That was what I was about to say. I know that."

"Good. I just wanted to make sure . . ."

"I know it. Okay? It is because I know it that this is going to be a tough conversation. I am going to have to talk in circles."

"Hey, Charlie. Talking in circles is what people like us do best."

Charlie knew that was right. And it made him feel sixty-four years old and tired and it made him want to go back to West Virginia to resume the life of a bed-and-breakfast operator. Just a few more minutes and maybe he could.

Charlie said: "All right, then. If someone came to you and said an official at the very highest level of the U.S. government fed information to the Soviets for several years in the late sixties and seventies, would that come as a shock to the Agency?"

"I cannot answer that."

"Because you do not know or for some other reason?"

"You're doing great so far, Charlie."

"Thanks, so are you. Would it be safe to assume that if there was such an agent in place at that time that the Agency or somebody else in the government knew about it?"

"I could not confirm what would be safe or unsafe to assume."

"If somebody you knew was about to make a decision of a life-or-death magnitude on that assumption, would you be in a position to raise one finger if the assumption was safe, two if it was not safe?"

Josh raised his right hand and then extended all five fingers.

"Thank you, Mr. Bennett, for nothing. The question that immediately comes to mind is, Why would the Agency let that kind of traitorous conduct go on without blowing a whistle from here to the heavens? It is a mystery to an ordinary citizen on the outside."

Josh said nothing. In the world of circular talk silence could mean everything or nothing. Charlie went on: "The ordinary citizen on the outside would then ask, Why? Why did the government not do something about this guy? There could be several answers. They did not know, they knew it but could not prove it or there was a high-level conspiracy and/or coverup of some bizarre kind that makes the eyes water even to think about . . ."

"My eyes are not watering, please note, Mr. Ordinary Citizen on the Outside, sir."

Now, what in the hell did that mean? Charlie decided to go for it. He had nothing to lose. The circular route had, like all normal circles, gone nowhere except back to where it began.

"Was he or wasn't he? is the question," he said. "You may signal your answer with your toes, an eyebrow swing to one side or another . . ."

"Okay, okay, okay. No more games. The answer is, I do not know. The files show all kinds of hints and charges but nothing definitive. Keep in mind I am not sure I have seen all of the files. But relax . . ."

"Relax? Come on, Josh. I cannot relax about this. Neither, god-damn it, should you."

"*Glasnost.* Have faith in *glasnost*, Charlie. Our people are already aching to get real access to the old KGB files. Nothing's happened yet but it's only a matter of time. If your man was working for the other side it will come out. That is assuming *glasnost* lasts, and I do not have to tell you there are some of our own people who have serious doubts about that."

Charlie had only two more questions.

"Why in the hell didn't you steer me right when I first asked you about him?"

"Because I didn't know it then. It was only after he had lunch with the old CI man that I got seriously curious. I went into those special files that only people with cosmic clearances and a lot of balls ever get to see. Some little tiny bits of it were in there. There wasn't enough to tell you anything and I wouldn't have anyhow. I still haven't told you anything. You told me. I am assuming he confessed to you and threw himself on the mercy of Charles Avenue Henderson . . ."

"What should I do about it?" Charlie asked. It was his last question.

"Nothing."

"Let the sonofabitch get away with it?"

"He won't. It will get out. Maybe after's he dead and gone if he's lucky, but it will get out. There's the *glasnost* possibility on the other side, but there's also one here. If I could get access to those little tiny bits in the records, others will, others probably already have. Somebody will talk, if it's only for historical reasons. The whole thing will be known, I promise you. And that includes your tiny little questions about who knew what and when and did what and when on our side."

Charlie said: "Come see us sometime in West Virginia, Josh. We'll treat you to eighteenth-century food, drink and ambiance."

"It's a deal. By the way, Charlie, McCone's daily work notes were in those files. I found a notation about what you and Clark told him about the assassination. Too bad nobody'll ever know about that. If you guys had gone the other way, there's no telling what might have happened."

Charlie said nothing.

"I've got one of my own right now, Charlie. I went all the way to the president with memos and in person to the National Security Council on Iraq. I told them two years ago to back off of Saddam. The man was a dangerous psychopath who couldn't be trusted. But we kept giving him what he wanted, letting him use agriculture credits to buy some dangerous stuff. Now look. Everybody thinks the intelligence was wrong. It wasn't and there's not a damned thing I can do about it, not a damned person I can tell."

They gave each other casual waves and left in separate directions.

━━━━━━

Charlie didn't even wait until he got back home. He went to a pay phone right there by the entrance to the lot where his car was parked. The call went through to Kermit Cushing.

"Mr. Clark always takes your calls, Mr. Henderson," said Cushing, "but he is not in yet this morning. I would suggest you call him at his apartment, but he said he did not want to be disturbed. He said he was ill. A stomach flu that's going around. I would be delighted to take a message."

Charlie thought about that possibility. Why not?

"All right," he said. "Tell him I called and left the following message:

> *Roses are red,*
> *Hearts are blue,*
> *To the Gods and glasnost,*
> *I leaveth you.*

"Will Mr. Clark know what this is in reference to?" asked Cushing.

"Yes, he will," said Charlie.

This is JIM LEHRER's ninth book, his seventh novel. He also writes plays. He is the associate editor of the *MacNeil/Lehrer NewsHour* on PBS and lives with his wife, novelist Kate Lehrer, in Washington, D.C. They have three daughters.

ABOUT THE TYPE

The text of this book was set in Janson, a misnamed typeface designed in about 1690 by Nicholas Kis, a Hungarian in Amsterdam. In 1919 the matrices became the property of the Stempel Foundry in Frankfurt. It is an old-style book face of excellent clarity and sharpness. Janson serifs are concave and splayed; the contrast between thick and thin strokes is marked.